THE SECRET WITCH

THE SECRET WITCH

By Jeff Severcool

ROWE BOOKS

Cover Art: Danielle Fine

Printed in the United States of America

First Printing, 2017

ISBN: 978-0-692-92882-0

Rowe Books
Mount Holly, NC 28120

www.jeffsevercool.com

My little love,

this was always for you

"This City pure is not for thee,
For things unclean there shall not be.
If I of Heav'n may have my fill,
Take thou the world, and all that will."

– The Flesh and the Spirit
        By Anne Bradstreet

"As a breath on glass, –
As witch-fires that burn,
The gods and monsters pass,
Are dust, and return.

– The Face of the Skies
By George Sterling

CHAPTER ONE

I lift my face toward Salem's sun, knowing fully well 'twill be one of the last warm afternoons of the year. My shoes scuff the road's loose stones as I stagger about, and the sky's fire searing between the clouds beckons me to look back down. However, I resist the urge, enjoying the orange light glowing deep through my squinted-shut eyes. The rest of my body suffers, hot and stifled under my wool dress, tucked and sweating under my bonnet, but my face remains free. Warm, sun-kissed, and free.

I feel a hand come up and brush my cheek, adding a slight guidance to the touch and bringing my view back down to the road.

I look over to see 'twas my sister Hope, who's now smiling at me.

"The prettiest part isn't the sun itself," she says, "but the power of its light. Instead, witness what it shows you, and take care not to trip please."

I look to my left and see my other sister Grace, swinging a basket about as if she's a young girl heading to school, not a woman about to be married. Though she is seventeen and two years older than myself, she has a way to her that suggests she is little more than a child trapped in a woman's body. And so it is, all three sisters walking from our orphanage to the village center so that her wedding can be prepared for, and she seems as if 'tis just another day. No cares and no worries at all.

Though we call each other sisters, we are not of blood and our common bond remains the lost histories written within our bones. Ones we'll surely never know. Hope is tall, slender, and fair with modestly sculpted features and the warmest brown eyes one could ever know. Grace is her exact opposite, much shorter than Hope and voluptuous everywhere, she rounds out even the most ill-fitting clothes with every curve of her body begging to show itself, and her wild blue eyes entice everyone from inside a frame of thick blonde hair.

"I honestly have no idea why they call it bundling," Grace says with one quick laugh. "There are no bundles of joy to be made with a large piece of wood between us." Never one to spare a moment of dramatic expression, she throws the back of her hand to her forehead and rolls her eyes as if she'll faint. "How terribly stupid is that?"

Hope smiles but doesn't look over to Grace, bearing no witness to her performance. "I'll assume it did not work very well, sister?"

Grace looks at Hope as if 'twas the dumbest question ever asked. "No, it most certainly did not." She smiles mischievously. "And all formalities aside, how do they honestly expect such a thing to prevent... such a *thing*?" She giggles at her own cleverness.

"I believe it to be a faith put in you two," Hope replies,

"that your vigilance will prevail even under the most tempting of circumstances."

I remain quiet, trying to understand exactly what 'tis they're talking about.

"That is not realistic whatsoever," Grace says, "for when the moon is high and all is dark and quiet, how does one forgo such a romantic opportunity?"

"I did not say it was easy to do." Hope looks over to her now, a captivating bit of seriousness upon her face. "But you must remember that marriage is far more testing than spending the night with someone properly, and *you* should be far more serious about it."

"Oh hush, stoic girl," Grace replies. "I may have had one night to myself, but you stay out suspiciously late at least once every week it seems."

Hope looks at her dismissively. "You know I have children to tutor those evenings."

"And I suppose if you returned home at a reasonable hour, that would disregard my suspicions. But you stay out quite late some nights—into the bundling hours I would say." She laughs loudly. "Who are you visiting, sister?"

Hope puts her hands on her hips and her aura becomes quite serious. "Don't you dare speculate about me in such a way. That is rather disrespectful and quite untrue of you to think of me in that manner."

Grace looks ahead for a moment. Her walk slows and the basket falls to her side, now swaying only with proper steps. It seems her boisterousness has subsided for now and maybe a bit of shame has fallen over her.

It becomes uncomfortably quiet for a long moment.

Hope looks to Grace and sees the fun has drained from her spirit. "It was quite funny, wasn't it? That day when John first came to ask Goodmother for your hand."

Grace's pouting face slowly shifts into a restrained smirk, but her eyes are bright again.

"I thought he was going to die right there," Hope continues. "He was saying his piece to her and then he noticed the blood all about her hands, for she had just lopped off five chicken's heads not a moment before he came to the house."

"Blood makes him so ill," Grace replies.

"I do believe he started to quiver." Hope smiles incitingly. "And oh *my* was he pale."

"How awful it must have been for him," Grace replies, "to be so apparently scared in front of us and Goodmother. He hasn't even spoken of it since."

"I hope you didn't cut yourself while bundling," Hope says. "That wood can be sharp and I'm sure it kept him a bit panicked through the night."

Grace smiles recklessly. "Nothing could have ruined that night sister."

We continue our walk into the center part of Salem. The mood in the air feels joyful and light, for the impending celebration of my sister's marriage seems to have given most of the villagers something to look forward to. My sisters decide it best to part ways with the discussion of Grace's midnight activities. Instead, the sounds of the square fill in around us as we arrive. The only lively bit of Salem Village is the square, and even so, lively is quite a strong word for the minimal amount of bustle. In the daytime hours, clopping horses and frolicking children move about the main road while the adults maintain the modesty of the village with head nods and well wishes as they pass each other by.

That is all that ever happens. Life here is so boring it makes me want to scream. And if doing something so improper wouldn't likely brand me a witch, I would. But such risks cannot be taken here, no matter how dreadful my life is. Salem's people love an execution and it does not take much 'tall to land yourself in the noose. I look over to the horrible platform where men and women alike have had their lives finished for them. Hangings are performed here with frightening regularity, yet nothing seems any better for them. I fear I'll never know why such barbaric acts were brought to this pure land.

We arrive to the center of the village, stopping together and looking at one another for an answer of what next to do.

"I have to go and meet with the minister," Grace says. "He's expecting me for marriage counseling. That leaves you two with the task of collecting food for the reception."

"Yes, sister," Hope replies. "Is there anything else that we can do?"

Grace has already started walking away but she whirls her head quickly over her shoulder and throws a big grin toward Hope. "Find yourselves a man to marry too."

Hope shakes her head, but she smiles. "Goodbye, sister. Have fun."

"Goodbye, my lovely bridgemaidens!" Grace yells back, not turning to look this time. She continues on, swaying her hips about and garnering as much attention as possible from the other village folk. She much enjoys being the object of people's fancy and will go to great lengths to stand out in a crowd, giving compliments to the women she passes by while bouncing for their men.

I turn to Hope. "What now do we do?"

"Well, we collect the offerings," she replies. "The minister is providing us a pig, so I put a barrel out in the Meetinghouse for those who'd like to contribute other items to the reception dinner. With how well-liked John's family is and how... popular Grace is, I'm sure the barrel has been filled with most everything we'll need." She takes my hand in hers and gives it a little squeeze. "Come now, this could take a bit of time."

A bit of time? How much could there be?

***

The door slams shut behind me at the beckon of my bottom and I stay resting against it for a moment, trying quite desperately to catch my breath. I move my arms up and down, bending at the elbow in a futile attempt to rid the horrible burn that has taken hold of my joints.

"Do they hurt much?" Hope asks, not looking up from her task of emptying the barrel.

"I'll be fine," I reply, still trying to remedy myself.

After an hour of lugging the barrel a mile back to the orphanage, our long table is now covered end-to-end with the most food I've ever seen. I scan down it while Hope pulls a few last potatoes from the bottom of her collection. Turnips, corn, squashes, and onions adorn the worn wood with delectable colors and boring potatoes fill in the gaps.

She throws the last couple onto the table, not caring where they land, and in one motion brushes her hair away and lets her hands fall onto her hips. "Well that's done." she throws on an exaggerated smile. "Ready to peel?"

"It has to all be done tonight?"

"That would be the best outcome, but if we have to do some in the morning, it'll be fine."

"I have to find her a gift yet."

"I'm sure having you there is enough Verity, and you're doing all this work as well."

"Yes, but you stitched her a beautiful dress for the occasion and I have nothing to offer."

"She has everything she needs," Hope replies, handing me a peeling knife. "I promise you this. Just attend, support her, and mostly, *humour* her. That's all Grace ever wants anyway."

I pick a potato and start carving the hard skin off in slivered circles, unearthing the moist, white untouched body. "I will think of something."

My hands move easily through their task and my eyes come up to the room around me. I think of all the times Grace and I played tag with one another around the very table I stand at now, bruising our hip bones on the corners of the sharp wooden ends as we ran clumsily around it. I look into the darkness of the common room behind me, over to the dead, unlit firestove. Grace and I would write out our dreams in the logs, using a knife to carve out the breathings of our hearts, and then we'd watch them burn away into smoke that escaped the orphanage prison. We would talk at night about how our dreams were out there, floating around the world. She believed someday they would manifest the creation of the life we desired. I still remember one of the first ones she ever wrote: *I want to be married.*

"We are sending her off into a new life," Hope says. "One where she is no longer an orphan, but a daughter in a new family. Gifts are nice, but what matters is that she knows how much we love her and how much good fortune we wish for her and her future."

"Pft," I slip. "How do I support that which I do not believe in?"

"With understanding."

"Oh, I understand," I reply, "I understand that marriages are dreadful legal ceremonies that steal my sisters away. I understand this quite well."

"Verity..."

"Do you even like him?" I slice in. "I don't and I *know* you don't either. He's worth nothing but his family's wealth. He's done nothing for himself, offers nothing. He's just a polished rock and Grace chose him! She is far too great for that man." I throw the knife onto the table. "Why would she ever say yes?"

Hope places her hand on my back and begins to rub in small circles. "Love is uniquely individual. Even if the whole world rejects the one you love, it changes not a bit of how you feel. Grace is happy now, Verity. I wish you could say the same."

Hope's touch has brought with it a calm that creeps through me. I feel myself relaxing, but I quickly resist and pull myself from her. I pick up the knife again and resume my potato task. I try to think of something else to talk about.

"What do you think Grace's counseling was about?" Hope asks, beating me to it.

"Proper conduct, proper dress, obedience to her husband…"

"So a whole list of things that Grace will not ever follow?"

"Can you see her actually being scolded by *John?*"

She shakes her head. "Never."

We both laugh together, but she quickly winces.

My eyes meet the spot where she's looking and I see blood running down her hand.

"Oh no, are you alright?"

"Yes, sister," she replies, wiping the blood onto her apron. "I suppose we musn't talk of Grace whilst we hold knives. We will likely laugh our fingers off."

She inspects the wound which quickly fills with blood again, but this time, she presses her hand into the apron, wrapping it around and holding it in place.

I watch my sister's blood coming through, staining the white fabric with a slow spreading of color, and before I know it, my mind becomes filled with the perfect idea for Grace's gift.

"Let's get your hand well," I say. "We have something important to do."

***

The briar bushes scrape my arms and cling to my sleeves as Hope and I press our way farther into the woods. Upon our wandering, we've collected many divers roots and dye berries which roll about in my carrying basket, but I'm certain we need more.

"Is this not yet enough?" Hope asks, sounding a bit out of breath.

My pace has been a quick march this far, but I slow a little, aware that she is tiring. My heavy steps become lighter and quieter, no longer dominating the sounds of our journey. The chirps and rustles of forest life come forth, and I slow down even more.

"How far have you explored?" I ask, turning back toward my sister.

She's staring at the ground and looks tired, but when she realizes I'm looking, she pains a smile upon her glistening face. "Hmmm, I don't think I've been *here* before."

"Well that's good, right? There's likely unharvested berries for us to pick."

"Maybe if thee pray," she replies, smirking at me.

"Prayers won't fill my basket," I say, swooping my free arm over my head. "Why, only these woods will." I let my arm fall back down to my side. "Maybe once you leave me too, I shall find how far they go."

"Leave you?"

"Yes, whenever you marry off like Grace."

She searches for words she cannot find but I relieve her of the burden.

""Tis alright, sister. I'll love you always, even when you go."

Hope looks first to the ground and then to the treetops. She brings her eyes back to me, but only for a moment. She turns away and looks far into the forest, as if she sees something terrible moving closer.

Something I see not.

"Please do not fret over this, sister," I say, bringing her back to me. "I wish to not waste this beautiful day with you."

Her eyes find the ground again and she sighs. "Shall we continue picking then?"

We walk on deeper into the forest, plucking any little red spots that we see amongst the brambles and tossing them into the basket. I peek inside of it and suppose that we are now close to having enough. Hope moves slowly however, and even though she's right behind me, she feels far away. Our thoughts laden the air around us, and I feel in my bones that whatever worries her 'tis more dreadful than usual concerns.

"Are you well?" I ask.

After a pause, she says, "with you I am."

"Would you tell me if something was wrong?"

The steady rhythm of branches snapping below our feet fills a longer pause that never leads to her response.

"Hope? Would y—"

"I would," she replies sharply.

"I may be younger than you, but I am not stupid."

She looks at me somewhat angrily. "Pardon?"

"You withhold secrets from me," I reply. "I've followed you before."

She halts. "You *followed* me?"

"Yes." My eyes avert from hers. "One night when you left for your weekly tutoring session, I waited a few minutes, and then I decided to follow a feeling I'd had for a while. A feeling that told me you weren't being honest with anyone. But no one else cares for you the way I do, so they never sensed the lie. I did."

Her eyes pierce me as if I am the betrayer. "When was this?"

"A couple weeks ago now." I shift my eyes off her for a moment and look around elsewhere. "I saw you meet with a man—a man I've never seen before in Salem. He was already waiting for you outside, keeping to himself across the road. You went to him and then you both walked on together. I did not see any more than this, and I didn't need to. I meant to ask you about him before, but there was never a good moment. Or maybe I just feared your answer."

She stares at me with defiance, as if I'm accusing her of something awful.

"I don't care to judge, I only worry, sister," I say, attempting to soften the confrontation. "Is he a lover?"

"No, he is not," she replies. "But not everything in my life is in need of your concerns and I'm done speaking about this. Let us get your berries and go home."

She turns away from me and starts quickly up through the woods. I hurry behind her with saddened thoughts and unfulfilled wonderings. Off to my right, I spot a bushel of red dots. I veer off the tiny path and push my way through a tangle of branches toward the berries.

"Over here," I yell to her, but before I can even finish the words, my feet slam into something solid, tripping me onto my palms and sending the basket and its contents scattered upon the piney ground. I roll over and am quickly greeted by a pair of black, glassy eyes. I let out a cry and jump to my feet, putting distance between myself and those eyes. But as I look again, I see the whole creature now — a dead doe lying across the forest floor.

As I look the animal over, my witnessing silence is interrupted by a lurching sound. I first think 'tis coming from the deer, but then I realize 'tis Hope. Standing behind me now, she has doubled over and turned away, but I know well what is about to happen. I let her be.

Turning back to the doe, something about its appearance strikes me peculiar. The deer I've seen hunted and brought back to the village for meat are always hefty creatures, plump and full. This one though is so thin and willowy, appearing less to be the body of a deer and more so the ghost of one.

I take a quick glance over my shoulder to check on Hope and it seems she has finished, standing upright now, but still facing away.

"Can I help you, sister?" I ask.

"No, I just need a moment," she replies quickly, so as not to incite any more sickness.

I notice something else strange when I turn back to the deer: two red spots against the earthy fur like berries against the woods. I move in closer, turning my head from side to side and allowing the light to come in at different angles.

They are puncture wounds.

Something with fangs killed this animal, yet did not eat it.

But why?

I stand, still surveying the creature, but I speak aloud to my sister. "Hope, I'm not sure if we should report this. 'Tis an odd and scary thing to find. I feel the other villagers would want to know of this."

She says nothing.

"Hope?"

I look over to where she was standing just in time to see her fall.

***

I run my needle through the fabric like a canoe cutting a gentle stream, looping and stabbing in tiny continuous circles. As I pierce the soft linen with the tiny dagger, I cannot help but notice how in harmony the pieces of my little task seem together. Before I had even begun, I had stared at the sections of snow-white cloth for minutes, holding the little weapon between my thumb and forefinger and figuring how best to begin its violation. Then I started into it, and now as the garter comes together, I can see the fruits of its death. A few stabbings have turned frayed cuts of fabric into a meaningful gift.

A gift that will remain for as long as the thread holds.

Goodmother would rightly have me killed if she ever found out where I acquired the garter fabric. I had searched everywhere I could think of for a sizable cut of white fabric, but there was nothing extra in the house. I had only one option: sacrifice a good linen. In my exasperation, I tore my bonnet from my hair and tossed it onto my bed. Just like that, I had the sacrificial cloth.

It was so perfect. The brim cut into three even strips would likely go most of the way around our legs and the remaining fabric could be cut into laces stitched to the garter. I would just tell Goodmother that I misplaced it and then suffer whatever punishment she sought fit to instill "responsibility" and "respect." To give my sisters these wonderful gifts was worth whatever reparations I would have to pay.

Purity's muffled voice cuts through the wall, but begins to clear as her words rise into shouts. Her and Goodmother have been discussing their concerns of Hope for the past hour and how likely 'tis that the impending wedding might be affected by the state of her health.

"This isn't fair!" Purity's shouts blister through the slits of space between the stacked logs of the wall between us. "I won't have it all ruined so Hope can maintain her beauty."

"And what exactly do you mean by this?" I hear Goodmother reply.

"What I *mean* is, Hope clearly hasn't been eating and the only reason I can think of for her to neglect herself in such a way is so she can remain thinner than myself. Even though I am the one that must tuck up into a dress on a day of display. *My* day."

"Halt your words right there," I hear Goodmother snap. "How dare you declare anything of the sort. This wedding has loosened your mind and I suggest you tighten it up because your sister is quite sick, and we know not why. She needs care and if your party must wait, it waits. I am certain the minister will heed my request of postponement."

After a pause, I hear Purity say something through the wall that I cannot quite decipher; something low and quiet. Something that precedes her stomping boots up the stairs to our bedroom, with a slamming of the door. I continue to listen for movement or voices. A moment passes and I hear the low groan of floorboards, indicating that Goodmother has settled into her sitting chair, not to rise anytime soon.

I continue my project, carefully inspecting each stitch for any crudity in the seam. I feel quite anxious and my hands move shakily over the cloth. I cannot stop worrying about Hope, for even when my mind is occupied with my work, worry still presses on the bottom of my belly like an unwanted stone, growing heavier with each minute. If nothing else in my life ever turns out well, I only ask for a grace of perfection in these garters, knowing they may very well be the last gift I ever give to my sisters.

And I ask that Hope is well.

My mind often gets the better of me, slamming the most detailed fears around inside of my head. Sometimes I think I'll go mad. Every day I spend here, I watch the people and the way they are. Their faces always look simple, never any indentations of worry lining their foreheads or sadness falling from their eyes; only indifferent folk passing each other on the way to indifferent tasks each day. I have to force myself to not let my feelings wash over my face. 'Tisn't wise to stand out in Salem. When people look at someone for too long, they begin to ask questions and here, 'tis very dangerous to be questioned.

I loop, knot, and tighten the final stitch, pulling it into a rigid line until it straightens, and I cut it close to the seam. I lay them onto the table, taking a moment to review my work. It looks as close to perfect as I'd expect to be possible and I get a brief feeling of satisfaction.

Now all that's left to do is to dip them red.

I collect the bowl of mashed dye berries and pour in a bit of water that has been sitting in a pitcher. The contents become a dark red pond, sinister in a way one would never expect of harmless berries. I carry the bowl carefully back to the working table when familiar sounds nearly cause me to drop it. A neighing horse, the popping of gravel under the weight of wheels – the doctor's carriage is here!

I quickly set the bowl down, sloshing a bit of red over the rim, and run into the other room. Goodmother has already risen from her chair and has taken position in the open doorway with her panicked hands at her mouth. I move behind her and shift myself into the area between her and the doorframe. The cold air moves around our bodies and into the house. Normally, Goodmother would be screaming at us to shut the door, but tonight, it seems to not matter to her one bit.

The carriage parks itself and the horse looks relieved, snorting into the air and then relaxing it's head toward the ground. The side door opens and Doctor Coverdale steps out. I do not see him much around the village, but when I do, all I can ever remember is how Grace always speaks of her affection for him. A clean man – intelligent, groomed, and with a self-assurance that can make dying patients feel comforted, I know he cared for my sister as well as he could. I see Hope glide herself to the edge of the seat. She places both feet firmly on the ground. Then with the doctor's assistance, she stands as well as she can. He moves behind her, one hand on her shoulder and one on her waist, and walks her step by step toward us. Hope looks up from her feet and her eyes meet mine. They look tired, but she smiles and mouths a "hello" to me.

My heart crumbles with joy. I move back into the house and pour her a cup of water, then I stand and wait impatiently for her to enter. I watch Goodmother move aside, and like a woman of royalty, Hope is guided delicately through the door and into the house.

I bring the water to her.

"Thank you, Verity," she says after a tiny sip. Her voice sounds weak.

Doctor Coverdale clears his throat and holds up a bag. "Ginger. Give her as much as she'd like and take care to monitor that she is drinking water all day. This should all pass soon."

"And as to the cause?" Goodmother asks.

"Unknown at this time," he replies. "But none too serious."

She looks at him the way she does when she knows we're lying. Her eyes penetrate for answers as she tries to extract them from whoever she throws her gaze upon. She smiles thinly, but her eyes don't change, so he averts his attention back toward his patient.

"Alright then, I'll be on my way now. If any other concerns arise or she shows fever, alert me immediately and I shall come as soon as I can."

Goodmother bows her head. "Thanks be unto you doctor."

"Thanks be unto you," I echo.

Without another word, he turns rigidly toward the door, exacting his steps like a soldier. He pulls his coat tightly around his chest and heaves the door open with one strong pull. The cold crashes around me, but lingers only for a moment after his departure. I go up to the door and press my body against it, ensuring 'tis latched, for there is a tendency for it to creep open in the night should it not be closed tightly enough, leaving us all to awaken with shivers.

Goodmother has taken Hope by the arm and has lowered her face, seemingly in an attempt to meet her gaze and lift it from the floor. Goodmother looks tendered. I never see her this way.

"Verity," she says without turning toward me. "Will you take Hope upstairs please? Walk her carefully and tend her needs with consideration of Doctor Coverdale's orders."

I walk to them with softened steps, as if somehow any noise would disturb her in this ill state even though it likely would not. I place my arm under hers, hooking at the elbow. This time, she looks up and smiles.

"I'm alright, sister," she says with a voice that sounds weak enough to suggest otherwise. "I'm only going to bed now. You can help me more tomorrow if you'd like. Maybe I'll make you my little servant girl and you can bring me tea all day and skip your bible lessons." Her eyes gleam with a humour brighter than her body can handle at the moment.

"That sounds wonderful," I reply. "I always wanted to be a servant. 'Twas my dream, you know – to bring people things."

We both giggle, but hers sounds more like breaths.

"Let me walk you upstairs at least," I offer.

"No need. I can walk," she replies. "They just keep pretending I can't. I only fainted. 'Tisn't that serious. Just a little ill at the moment. All will be well soon enough."

There is unsteadiness in her words – validations spoken to me, but meant for herself.

"Goodnight, Verity," she says. "Come rest up soon. We have a wedding tomorrow." She starts up the stairs, halting any further discussion for tonight.

"Goodnight, Hope," I reply. "I'm finishing up Grace's gift, but it won't take me long."

"Alright then." Her voice carries down the stairs, but she's already to the room. I hear the door creak open and then shut with a loud click, punctuating the otherwise silent house.

Everyone has retired to bed except myself. It upsets me that Grace didn't come down to greet Hope, but perhaps the wedding ordeals have left her exhausted. Or 'tis possible she didn't hear us, for her room is at the very end of the upstairs hall. Even though Hope is the oldest of us girls, Grace was the one that threw fits over wanting her own room after 'twas just the three of us left here at the orphanage. I never said a word against her wishes. I need Hope with me at night. Hope never objected either, because she knew that I did.

With the commotion over and everyone in their rooms, I find my way back to my project. I snatch the nearest rag to clean up the contents that have sloshed onto the table. The rag soaks the liquid up off the wood, leaving behind the faintest stain. I unfold it and hold it like a sheet in front of my face, inspecting the quality of the dye. The cloth is striped a perfect red – colorless only in the creases where 'twas folded in my hand.

I grab up the garters and dip them into the bowl, carefully pinching the laces and keeping them white and out of the dye while the rest of them bathe in crimson. One of them slips from my grip and falls completely under. I fish it out with my left hand while my right holds the other two tightly in position. I collect the submerged garter and hold it above the bowl until the dripping slows. When I feel the moment is right, I run into the next room, shoulder the back door open, and immediately kick it shut behind me. The cold of the quiet night strikes my body and brings shivers through my bones.

I walk around the side of the house with my arms outstretched and the wind grips my wet hand, turning it to ice. I find the drying line and carefully tie the ribbon of each one into a tight knot around it, ensuring they won't blow away. The moonlight washes over my skin as my fingers finish their task. I raise them up into the light. One is pale and pure, but the other looks as if it has been streaked in blood. Mirror images of life and death.

The treeline behind my hands catches my attention and I lower them back to my sides as my eyes go far into the darkness of the woods. I think of the deer we found earlier and the strange circumstance of its death and only one thought emerges to consume all of my wonderment.

There is something quite scary in that forest and I want to know what it is.

CHAPTER TWO

One glance around the chapel suggests that this wedding is going to be an odd affair. The attending men and women have forgone their black clothes for varying hues of faded pastel colours, like a congregation of dismal flowers trying their best to look pretty. The air is quite restless and everyone shifts about.

I've saved Hope a place next to me on the pew, for she hasn't yet arrived. Doctor Coverdale was just pulling up to the orphanage as Goodmother and I were leaving. 'Twas simply a necessary follow-up and he seemed confident that she would be well. I had spoken with her this morning and she seemed herself again, much to my relief.

A low groan and a long creak turn the heads of the adults toward the back of the chapel. A shape moves through the door with a bowed head – 'tis Hope! She's followed by Doctor Coverdale and his wife Goody, who enter with a prestigious air about them, as if my sister is a presentation of their great achievements in medicine.

She lifts her eyes and a small wave from me is all it takes for her to notice, smile, and make her way over. She slides in next to me and gives me a quick hug. I instantly feel complete again. I'd been so worried about her that I hadn't slept at all, allowing exhaustion and anxiety to beat a terrible feeling into my body. She had slept the whole night through, and I laid there straining to hear her breaths – to assure myself she was fine. Sudden deaths here are not uncommon, and my thoughts always fall on the worst that can happen, never the best.

"How are you feeling?" I ask.

"I feel well," she replies with a smile. "I told you not to worry about me sister."

"I know, but I couldn't help myself," I say. "Did the doctor give you any further instructions?"

"Yes, he said to stay out of the scary woods."

"Did you tell him of the deer?"

"I did," she replies. "I suppose normally the ministry would want to know, but I think 'tis more sensible to speak to a man of science first."

I look around me; sternly blank faces in all directions. "I'm certain you're right. What did he say?"

"Not much, but he seemed concerned by it." She puts a hand to my face. "You didn't sleep a bit, did you?"

"Not a bit," I reply. "Is it that apparent?"

"No, my pretty. I just know your face too well."

A side door opens at the front of the chapel, pulling our attention to an elder who makes his way to the pulpit. He removes his hat, revealing a scalp full of matted, but thinning hair. He looks around at us all with expressionless, sunken eyes. For his position as the bringer of people's wedding dreams, he hardly looks the part.

"Well someone had to make sure you weren't going to lay a postponement on Grace's wedding because of poor health," I say, turning back to her.

Only she's not listening. She is rigidly fixated on the elder as if she was a doe that just heard a twig snap in a silent forest.

I touch her hand. "Hope?"

This time she turns to me, shaking away a bit of glassy fear from her eyes. "I'm sorry, dear. What is it you were saying?"

I want to ask her what's wrong, but the elder is looking expectantly to the congregation now, waiting for us all to settle the rustling and low chatter occupying the space of the room.

"Nevermind," I reply. "We'll talk later."

Her eyes stay on me for a moment. They brim with a concern that brings age to them, like deep seas of wisdom she's gained at a heavy cost. She looks away from me, knowing I'm trying to pull from her whatever 'tis she's hiding.

The elder clears his throat and begins. "O, Blessed be this morning to you all. I dispense on behalf of God the tidings of a ceremony above the civil custom of union that Salem has seen before this day. For it is the adjudication of our new minister to restore our lord once again to his rightful place as the one true overseer of all matrimonies conducted here. While our church remains governed under the ministry delegations of Salem Town, they have allowed us to further advance our church participations by electing a temporary minister for the village. In our best efforts to cultivate a community of theocratic devotion, it is my pleasure to announce the arrival tomorrow of our new minister, Lazarus Barrowe."

The audience perks up into decries. Men shout about things

that I do not understand. Things related to doctrines and compensation issues – things yet unresolved. I've never concerned myself with village matters. I'll either leave here or die, so I never felt as if I should need to join the fervor that grips everyone else.

The elder continues, "Reverend Barrowe has held the position of elder in Salem's parish for a many number of years and 'tis with great respect that we wish thee well as he leads us into a new place of righteousness. His term length is undecided at this time, but we hope to resolve our independence from Salem Town within a few seasons." He steps out from behind the pulpit and moves closer to us, relaxing his posture and rubbing his hands together as if about to eat a delectable meal. "Now, let us commence with the ceremony that we've all gathered for today. Usher, bring in those who are to be wedded."

The large back doors to the meetinghouse's chapel open slowly, revealing my beautiful sister standing hand in hand with her husband-to-be. She's wearing the dress Hope had made and though the seams have snugged into her a bit more since the last time she tried it on, everything about her looks *right*. I try to catch her eyes, but she stares off into things not residing in the chapel. She stares into the future she likely never thought would be: her dream coming true. When you're an orphan, 'tis very easy to believe that no one would ever want you and every time she looks at John, her eyes glitter as if she's found the impossible.

"Groom-to-be and his bride," the elder says, "come forward now and take your place at the altar."

Grace and John make their way to the front in perfect unison, as if they've practiced this. When they meet the elder at the altar, he motions for them to face each other and they abide.

The elder has shifted his focus from the crowd unto them. His eyes move back and forth between Grace and John as the celebratory smile falls slowly solemn. "At the beginning God created man and woman so that two could be joined as one. One inseparable flesh. What God has joined together, let no one separate."

I look back over to Hope for a moment. Concern still haunts her face. I try to push it from my mind and concentrate on my sister's wedding, but I hardly can in the midst of her apparent worry.

The elder motions for them to join hands. "A wife of noble character is worth far more than rubies. A wife of noble character is her husband's crown. But a disgraceful wife…" he looks directly into Grace's eyes, "is like a decay in his bones."

I notice Hope's head drop and she stares at the floor for a moment. She seems to be recollecting herself, murmuring silent things and rubbing her hands together. She brings herself to look back up.

The elder moves his eyes back out toward the congregation. "Do not let the transgressions of harlots overshadow the beauty of today, for these two will spend many faithful years together. But do heed when I say that the lord's law will be enforced to the harshest standard under our new minister. Now be imitators of God, therefore, as dearly loved children and live a life of love, just as Christ loved us and gave himself up for us as a fragrant offering and sacrifice to our father. Remember this day, remember these times, rejoice in your youth and if sin occurs inside your union, turn toward the church and confess any wrong-doings so that your marriage may become clean again." His eyes narrow gravely as he lets out a sharp cough, scanning over everyone like a hawk searching for any little sign of a rat. "Now today is one of celebration, but the moment of having you all gathered must not be spared, for danger and evil seems to have found its way into our land." He slams his fist down on the pulpit, startling everyone. "There is a witch among us. A demon. An entity of evil that feasts on the blood of our animals. Something is living in our woods, invited here by the unholiest of us. I know not what it is, but I know that we must remain devout in our godliness to dispel this darkness from our village. Pray and beg for mercy and do not fall into darkness yourselves. For its next feast may be one of our children." After a long pause staring out into the faces of stunned and frightened villagers, he appears to realize the inappropriateness of addressing this matter during a wedding. He resumes his position once again of composure; hands gently clasped, straight posture, and the slightest smile. "Now, while I'm sorry for speaking of devilish things during this time of union, it is imperative to the safety of our community that we ruin through vigilance, any chance that Satan may have to claim this land from us and God. We will honour this subject at a later date when we have more information to give you all. But for now, let us resume in our acknowledgment of *this* occasion." He holds his hands out toward Grace and John.

The radiance that had been so apparent in Grace's face has dulled under the words of the elder, for he talks so much of sin and hardly of joyousness on a day that is supposed to be a celebration of love. I feel bad for her, but I know today will be soon forgotten as she starts her new life.

A while passes and the rest of his droning moves far beyond me, just as all sermons in this place do. My thoughts stay on his talk of other animals being killed in demonic fashion. What else has been discovered? Everyone sits and patiently listens, waiting for the formalities to come to their end. Eventually, the elder parts between the couple and steps closer to us – a sign that he's about to conclude. "Now, on this Saturday, the first of October, sixteen forty four, I pronounce these two husband and wife under God and the government of Salem. The finalization of matrimony is one of legalities and signatures and no longer requires the presence of you all. You may go and tend your homes for the rest of the afternoon, but return at sunset for the dinner celebration. It will be one to remember. Thanks be unto you all."

The sounds of everyone moving at once rises into the air. Pew benches creaking from lifted weight, low conversations, and general commotion grows while people leave slowly, enjoying their bit of talking time together. Normally I would be the first one out of the chapel, shaking myself clean in the fresh air, but a quick look around suggests that I will not be the first to leave today.

Hope is gone already.

***

I've not witnessed a time when the men and women of Salem are permitted to act as loose and foolish as they are right now. Outside, women whirl their dresses in dancing circles as men clap and jump around them over the stomps and table beating of the reception's guests. Some man I do not know plays a lute that the church had kept in storage since it first came over by ship. For as long as I've been alive, music has been largely forbidden with the exception of hymnal singing but tonight, it seems the festivities have possessed everyone into rare gleeful madness.

The elder had explained to everyone that since no minister has been officially instated with accompanying governing bodies, tonight would be a true celebration with dancing, music, and drink permitted for all. He said that tonight, God would laugh at our foolery. I don't think 'tis funny though. I find it all quite obnoxious.

I've chosen a spot off in a corner far enough away to keep me from getting caught in the swell. My eyes travel from face to face, trying to spot Hope. After the service was done, I'd gone back to the orphanage to collect all of the food we'd prepared, but she was not there. In fact, she never returned. I wanted to tell Goodmother, but I chose not to, knowing that my sister would be in much trouble whenever she *did* find her way to the reception.

I leave my post outside of the madness and move through the raucous crowd to get myself a cup of cider. Passing Goodmother on the way, I slink by and hear her talking of me with another woman.

"Verity is a strange one," Goodmother says. "It would

require a true act of God to place her with a man who could ever tolerate the eccentricities and moodiness that she would bring to a marriage."

The woman responds, "But she's quite beautiful, unlike any other of Salem's girls."

"She's frail," Goodmother says. "She never eats."

That's because your cooking is horrid.

I keep moving until I reach the large tables that remain adorned with food and drink. The feast is actually quite engaging. I had helped set everything up, but while working, I didn't get to appreciate the display. Under the setting sun however, the arrangement of fruit and stews contained in all the best pottery the people have to offer looks rather marvelous.

I grab a mug and lift the lightest pitcher, pouring whatever cider is left into my cup. As I set it down, hands slam onto the table next to it, startling me enough to slosh some drink onto the ground. Grace smiles at me, panting from all the dancing and eyes blazing with excitement.

"Why hello there, sister!" she says. "Are you not going to dance tonight? Have the festivities not enlightened you to the wonders of matrimony? We must find you someone to dance with so we can start you on your way. Come!"

Before I have a chance to respond, she whirls up my arm and plants me in front of the first boy she can find that's my age. He's timid looking with long ashy hair tied behind his head and he seems just as surprised as I.

"Hello there, young man," Grace says. "This is my sister, Verity. And you are?"

He pauses for a moment before replying, "Thomas."

"Thomas, eh?" she says. "Strong, biblical, and sincere. I love it." She grabs our hands and brings us closer to one another. "I think it wise that you two dance and acquaint. I shall return soon." She grabs his face with both hands, squeezing it into a pucker and giving him an exaggerated kiss on the cheek. She does the same to me and then leaves us, disappearing back into the heart of the party.

"I'm sorry for her," I say. "She's a bit much."

"'Tis alright," he replies. "She seems fun."

"Fun?"

"Well, she seems *happy*."

"Yes, well, she's always that way."

Grace has a way of bending the world whenever she needs it to. Whatever she wants, she gets—usually sooner rather than later too. Quite a remarkable quality 'tis, to be so strongly minded that your very aura seems to shift everything around you so that it perfectly fits your needs. I will probably never understand how she does this. How she never suffers over anything.

"How old are you?" he asks.

"Fifteen."

"As am I." He shifts around nervously, playing with the hem on the bottom of his coat tails. "You and your sister are from the orphanage, yes?"

"We are."

"Is it nice there?"

"Not really," I reply. "I have a room, no parents, and one less sister."

"One less?"

"Only my sister Hope is left there with me. The other was married today."

Her name slams into me. For a moment, I'd become distracted enough to let her disappear from worry, but more time has passed and she still hasn't shown. Now I'm more worried than before.

"I *have* parents," he says, "but I don't like them very much."

"I don't like anyone very much."

"Do you like me?"

"I suppose you're tolerable." I crack the smallest bit of smile so as not to hurt his feelings. Though he is, I wish I could be alone again. I have never been one to enjoy acquainting myself with strangers.

"Do you think you'll marry?" he asks.

"No."

The word sounds so short and final that for a second, I almost regret saying it. But some things don't require explanation. Sometimes we feel the weight of one word more certainly than many.

"You don't think you'll find someone to love?"

"I'm not looking for love," I reply. "I'm looking for other things."

"But if you become sick, who will care for you?"

"If I become sick, I will just sleep until I get well or die."

"And what of children then? You do want children, aye?"

"I don't need marriage for a child."

"But if you are unwedded…"

"Only in Salem," I reply. "There are many places in this world where things are not run like they are here."

"And you intend to see them?"

"I do."

He looks at me strangely, as if mentioning other parts of the world is to speak of fantasies. He also looks sad.

"Have I disappointed you, Thomas?"

"I just don't understand."

"'Tisn't your job to."

An awkward silence passes between us and even though I want to run away, I feel frozen by obligation to be polite to this boy. I take a sip of my drink which turns into a gulp, buying some time away from our conversational discomfort.

"You should try the cider," I say, wiping my mouth.

"I have," he replies. "I loved it." He looks even more nervous now than before. "I also love your dress. It looks... well made."

His words shock me. I look down quickly at my dress to see what he could be talking about. 'Tis a faded brown color that looks more like a rag and less like formal wear. To compliment it in any way is to make no sense at all. "Thank you Thomas, but I think your eyes deceive you."

"No, I think you look wonderful."

Another silence falls between us, but somehow less awkward than before. I don't have long to ponder it, for I am suddenly swooped away by someone who has whirled behind and collected me into their dance. I'm whipped around to face my kidnapper.

"Hope! Where have you been?"

"I'll return her!" she shouts back toward Thomas.

"I wasn't sure you'd come at all," I say. "'tis late."

"I didn't mean to cause you concern," she replies, "but this whole wedding had me more emotional than I ever thought would happen. I just needed to be alone for a bit."

"No, something else is going on," I say. "I don't know what, but I saw you in service today."

"You saw what?"

"You just looked... worried or something."

"I *was* worried. I wasn't quite feeling myself yet and I was afraid I would throw up in the middle of Grace's wedding."

"Are you sure that is all?"

"That is all."

She swings me around a bunch, but I'm not really dancing. I feel like she's simply attempting to show that she's physically better, but I'm not willing to accept that as the whole story. I know there is something she's still not telling me.

"This reception is quite marvelous, is it not?" she asks, finally halting and releasing my hands on account of my very obvious detest of dancing.

"It's everything Grace wanted I'm sure," I reply, adjusting my ruffled dress into place again.

"Have you spoken with her yet?"

"Not really," I reply. "She came and planted me in front of that boy and left us. I haven't seen her since."

"I saw her for a moment," she says. "She's already speaking of having children. I'm hoping 'tis only drunkenness talking, but can we know?"

"She *is* a child," I reply.

We both giggle and the tension falls away. I suppose we all struggle with things sometimes and if Hope has something bothering her that she wishes not to share, she is entitled to her secrets. She looks well, and that is all that really matters.

"Oh look, here comes the maiden of the night herself," Hope says, gesturing an open hand toward Grace, who is trotting to us.

"Hello, sisters," Grace falls in with us looking quite disheveled. "Is this not the greatest night ever put on by Salem Village?"

"To the one who has had considerable drink, I must agree," Hope replies.

Grace laughs. "I'm not a drunker."

"You're a tipper," Hope says.

"A tipper?" Grace furrows her brow.

Hope reaches out to grab both of Grace's shoulders, straightening her up. "You were tipping, my dear, but you are straight and narrow once again."

We laugh together and for a moment, I'm the happiest I've ever been. Tonight is quite possibly the last time the three of us will get to spend together this way. Grace's life is about to change forever and she will not be permitted time away from her duties to folly with orphans.

The village sees only what it wants to see, and to Salem, we are not real sisters. Our sisterhood was granted as a way to survive not having a family of our own; always meant to be temporary and revocable once we became married off.

"Hold a moment," Grace says. "I'll be right back."

She wanders off through the crowd again to the ale table. Hope and I watch as she pours three cups, collects them together awkwardly with her hands, impressively lifts them, and makes her way back to us all without getting bumped.

"Perhaps she's not as drunk as I thought," I say.

Hope smiles at me before Grace rejoins us.

"What are you smiling about?" she asks. "Do not be making fun of tippers now. Not on their wedding day." She holds the cups out to us. "Here, take one, ladies."

We each collect one from our grasp. I put my nose over the rim to smell the contents. There is an odour that is both pungent, sweet, and otherwise not inviting at all.

Grace walks toward the woods and more into the shadows. She stops when it seems we are covered and far enough away from the touching light of the hung lanterns.

"A toast to our sisterhood," Grace says, raising her cup before her. "To our bond, our love, our family of three." She then looks at Hope, telling her with a glance that she must say something now.

Hope looks a bit ill—perhaps the smell of the ale bothers her as it does me. But she raises her cup as well. "To the loveliest woman who never ceases to remind her two more serious sisters what it means to be without care. Who always keeps us laughing, who we love so very dearly, and who we wish to be only with joy in her new life."

Grace gets a bit teary, her large pretty eyes glimmering in the flickers of light that cut through to us. "Hope, that was so beautiful." She wipes away a stray tear. "And you, Verity?"

I use my free hand to reach into my dress where I've tucked away the garters I've made. "I have a gift. For both of you."

My sisters look at each other in honest surprise.

I remove the little crimson garters and hold them out in offering. "Take one."

They both reach forward and untangle them from one another, leaving just one left in my hand.

"They are garters I've made. I've scarletted them with dye and they are a symbol of who we are. We are not like everyone else here. We are cast-aways. We are orphans. We are blood sisters even when they say we are not, and we will never submit ourselves completely to a life without a little bit of rebelliousness. I love you both more than anything else in this world or after. I hope you wear this always and remember that no matter what happens, our spirits are forever entwined and these garters are a symbol of our eternal sisterhood. Salem cannot break us apart."

Grace's eyes bear down on me with an earnestness that she did not even give to her husband in ceremony. I cannot remember her looking at me this way before. "Verity, I do not know what to say. I am quite shocked in the best of ways right now. To hear you speak this way... you no longer sound like my little sister. You are a woman now." She raises her cup again that has drifted down in her gifted surprise. "To sisters then. Blood sisters."

I look over at Hope and her lip is trembling; she is fighting hard to keep back tears.

"Hope! I did not mean to upset you."

"I'm not upset," she says between sniffles, "just touched."

"Drinking helps with rampant emotions, sister," Grace says. "Let us toast quickly and we can all cry together."

Grace throws her head back and lets the liquid fill her throat with a face of savored satisfaction. I try to do the same, but the burn causes me to cough and my head snaps forward just in time to see Hope toss the contents of the cup with a quick wrist flip and then pretend to drink.

All the worry that had left me creeps back into my stomach once again.

***

The rest of the evening was quite droll. Eventually, it ceased to even *be* a reception any longer. The villagers became far too drunk. Their dancing slowed, their bodies retired to benches, heads hit the tables, chill overtook the air, and all that was left were ravaged food baskets, tipped pitchers, and sober folk trying to collect their drunken loved ones for a laborious walk home.

Hope had left ahead of me. She was obviously tired, but a bit more concerning was how quiet she'd gotten after I'd given her and Grace their garters. She went home shortly after that and left me wondering if I'd somehow upset her. Grace told me not to worry and then proceeded to explain all the things about Hope that I already knew.

"She's sensitive, Verity," she had said. "After all, I almost cried because of those wonderful gifts."

I contented myself with Grace's explanations and politely agreed with everything she said until her husband came to collect his bride with an eager, drunken grin. They left and I decided I should as well.

Walking home now, I slow myself, enjoying the solitude of the chilly night. I kick loose stones in the otherwise quiet street, thinking of how lonely the house will be with Grace gone. She annoys me so much, but I miss her already.

Something rustles on top of a building and shrieks, causing me to jump. I look up toward the sounds, catching sight of an owl that glides off away from our village and into the woods. I wonder if it witnessed the strange death of the deer we found. They say that owls are the wisest of creatures. Maybe it knows what happened.

I've never been one to believe in anything beyond our world. The fears of ghosts and devils that plague others have never captured me. But the instance of the deer is quite odd and a bit frightening. I know of no such animal that leaves the meat behind, only drinking of the blood. Maybe there *is* something out there to be worried about.

When I arrive home, I slide my hand over the icy latch and try, with great difficulty, to gently open the door. The cold has helped seal it shut and I'm forced to slam myself into it, for it will not budge otherwise. The door bursts open behind the bit of force I was able to levy upon it. I shut it behind me with a swift push that is quieter than expected in the stillness of the house.

The house is cold. I think I see my breath but 'tis too dark to be certain. I kick my boots off near the door and pad my way across the freezing wooden floor to the stairs. I tip-tap quickly up them and open my bedroom door. I fully expect to hear Hope breathing deep and slow like she does every night, but instead I hear a whisper.

"Verity."

"Hope?" I reply. "What are you doing awake?"

"Waiting for you."

I climb into my bed next to her and wrap myself in the icy

sheets, curling my body into a tight ball until my warmth begins to overtake the bed.

"Come over here. My bed's already warm," she says.

With no hesitation, I throw the covers off and run over to her bed. She lifts the sheets like a cloak and I climb into the space, which she quickly closes around me once I'm snuggled in.

We're both quiet for a moment, reveling in the warmth and comfort of each other.

"I miss Grace," I say.

"As do I."

With Grace gone, the reality of my life falling away has become all too real. When Hope leaves, I'll have lost everyone I love forever.

"Now what will become of you and I?" I ask.

"I believe we shall both live, love, and die, my little one," she says, answering my question with a perspective larger than I'd intended.

"I don't want to die."

"Why not?"

"Why is that the way? What is the point? There is no point. Life is just one big nightmarish lie and Salem only adds to the misery every day."

"Well, if life is the nightmare, maybe death is the dream," she replies. "I think there is magic we cannot see."

I sigh and roll away from her, facing the colder side of the bed and saying nothing, but my thought is clear: *nonsense*.

"Why do you always bring this up at night, sister?" she asks softly.

I wallow in my stubborn silence for just a moment before setting it aside in lieu of Hope's comforts. "Because I'm scared."

Every night is the same for me. I lie in restless pondering of death and I can never turn my thoughts toward anything else. I feel my heartbeat, knowing one day it will cease. I become painfully aware of my breath, my eyes, my head, my legs. I stare into the darkness, too present for my own good. I recount the stories I've heard, the hangings I've watched, the burials I've been to, the passages I've read. I swirl all these memories together and I dwell about my own death.

Every single night.

"I don't think fear is right," she says. "You only fear it because the outcome is uncertain. I think death could be the most magical experience ever."

"Rotting in the earth doesn't seem very magical to me."

"Oh how morose of you, Verity," she says. "Think beyond the crudity and dream beyond the fear. All could be so perfect on the other side of this fragile life. Maybe once we shatter, we awaken."

"Like heaven?" I dismiss.

"Maybe, maybe not. Maybe *better*."

The stubbornness inside of me tightens and it proves difficult to accept any of Hope's invalidated words, though I feel her love behind them. Talking to her eases me even when I feel like I gain nothing more from our discussions. In the silence of the night, when fear consumes every thought, her words are a warm embrace.

"Verity," she says. "I need you to know that my love for

you exists between this all. It shines brighter than light, it is more abundant than the collective drops of every rainstorm, it is purer than an untouched snowflake. It lives between and around and beyond everything worldly because it isn't something of this world, and I do believe it will always remain. Life and death as you think of them are only relevant to our bodies. Death does not apply to love. Some things truly are eternal, and so our love shall always remain."

"Until you leave me," I reply.

Her hand comes over my face, slides some hair aside, and brushes my cheek in a slow rhythm. I feel my body relax, my mind soothe, but tears well in my eyes. I know I won't have this forever.

"I'm not leaving you."

"You will."

"No," she replies. "*We* will."

I untuck my head out from under her chin and look up into her eyes, brightened even in the dark. "We?"

"If you'd fancy it," she says. "Do you want to leave Salem with me?"

I roll over and face her, searching her eyes for every bit of sincerity. I almost feel guilty for doing so; Hope has never lied to me. Her words are always devout.

"To where?" I ask.

"I was fancying England," she replies, "but of course you'd also have a say in the matters of our destination."

"I've dreamed of England!" I find her hands under the covers and grab them, squeezing with uncontrollable excitement. "I feel hopeless here, like there was never anything for me. I wish to explore cities like London, where there is so much *more* – more people, more bustle, more possibilities. Yes, sister. England 'tis."

"England 'tis," she echoes with relief.

"When shall we leave?"

Her eyes move from me and about the room, taking it all in, and I feel her answer before she can speak it. "Tonight."

Adventure penetrates me, but worry follows close behind. Hope is not the type to ever act drastically. She is calculated and serious about her decisions. She plans everything so carefully, even her bible lessons. I would always choose at random something from the book to explain about in class, wanting nothing more than to get it over with, but Hope would spend hours studying the texts, needing to find the perfect passage.

"How would we leave tonight?" I ask. "We haven't even packed. Where would we go?

"There's a passenger ship leaving early tomorrow morning at four o'clock," she replies. "The records room at the meetinghouse keeps an inventory of shipping times arriving and departing from Boston. I verified these with the man you saw me meet with and I paid him already for both of us to board one leaving for England. 'Tis why I was late to the reception. But it has to be now, for the next one doesn't leave again for at least a month."

"Why didn't you tell me?" I ask. "You were going to leave me here, weren't you? Had I not confronted you about your secret affairs, you would have left me behind."

She looks away. "I was."

Hurt stabs my heart while tears erupt into my eyes. "I cannot believe you would do that to me. Who *are* you?"

"I had no choice, Verity." She grabs my face in both of her hands and stares deeply into my eyes. "There are dark and dangerous things happening here. Things that no one is aware of. There is no time to explain now, but I will tell you everything once we are safely on the boat. I had planned to find someone of authority in Boston to report what I know, but I couldn't risk you getting caught too. I was going to write you from England when everything had been resolved, and I was going to request that you join me. I would never leave you, Verity. Never."

"Why then did you offer me to join you tonight?"

"Because I believe you won't make it here," she replies. "I feel the depths of your sadness, and I realized that leaving you in that way may push you too far. I worried you'd have hurt yourself to escape this maddening village at any cost before any of my letters could reach you. Or worse, I feared that those responsible for the terrible things I know would come and hurt you instead of me."

"You're scaring me."

"Well, let us waste no more time tonight," she says. "Leave whatever isn't necessary and let us be on our way."

My eyes search the room while my mind scatters itself over what I need to bring. I'm still wearing my good dress, not yet changed from the reception. I decide 'twill do. I fetch my wool coat, believing the open seas to be rather cold. I also claim socks and some other garments laid upon one another. How does one prepare for a journey like this? I look over to Hope, deciding to mirror her approach. She's holding nothing, but is now wearing a heavy coat as well.

"Let us leave," she says. "Whatever else we need we can get in Boston before we board. I have money."

Money? From where? It doesn't matter now. I'll ask her later.

We break for the door together, but the sounds of horses outside halt us as we open it.

"Do you hear that?" I ask.

She remains quiet, but her eyes rise with sheer terror. "Get in the bed."

"Why?"

"Do it, Verity! You must listen to me! Take your clothes off quickly. They cannot know that you had part."

I tear my dress down as the boom of the front door being slammed open shudders the house. I jump into my bed and try with everything in me to cease my trembling. Hope does nothing. Even as the boots stomp up the stairs and the riotous voices grow louder, she stands in front of the door like a ghost, waiting for the men to enter and pass right through her. She turns back to look at me. I see a thousand apologies in her eyes, but the fear is gone.

"I'm sorry, Verity," she says. "I love you."

The door breaks open and two men push in side by side, followed by three more and a terrified Goodmother, who is denied entry and pushed back into the hallway.

"Hope Bridgemaiden," one of them announces in a voice that's strikingly loud. "Thou hast been declared arrested by order of Salem on charges of heresy and sexual immorality."

Two of the men grab her by each arm and direct her toward the door.

"Sentencing will follow a civil trial given tonight with considerable input from the ministry." He unfolds a yellowed piece of paper in his hands and stares at the document for a moment. "After sentencing has been lain, thou are to be confined to the stocks due to the particularly sensitive nature of the crime, and to thus avoid the possibility of spreading witchery unto common folk residing in the public jail."

One of the men stares me down. "And of this one, sir?"

Hope drills her eyes into the man with the paper. "She knows nothing of this. I've told her nothing."

He nods in approval. "Fine then, leave her be," he says to the men. "If she too is a witch, such will be revealed in time and execution will swiftly follow, but for now, let us be on our way. The trialmen await us."

She is rushed from the room, but the door stays open and hollow as the noise of the men fades down the stairs, out the door, and off into the night.

***

"There's magic in this world."

When those words fell from her lips, I knew somewhere in my heart that they would be the last she would ever speak to me.

Sure that tonight would be her final night of confinement, I had pattered as quietly as I could across the loose stones of the open midnight road and into the square where the townspeople would gather by day to witness whatever announcements the political men of Salem Village had to offer.

The announcement, made this afternoon, was that Hope

Bridgemaiden had been sentenced to die by hanging at 10 o'clock tomorrow.

When I had gotten to the platform, her hands were limp and bent out of the wooden trap holes like two wilted tulips. Her matted head hung heavily from the stocks like dead iron against the evil oak closure and blood dripped down from somewhere near her neck. The autumn leaves had begun to fall days before, content to stay on the ground. Until tonight. Tonight they came alive and swirled around her devilishly, mocking her in crisp circles and dancing free in the wind while her life withered away in confinement.

Then the wind went on and the leaves fell quiet again.

She had been left atop the stockade platform to rot like a gourd and three days had passed now. 'Twas there alone where she suffered sunrise to sunset, ridiculed and cursed and spat upon by the monsters of this town. Then night would fall and the cursing ones would retire home to be surrounded by warm food and warm families – laughing, good stories, children, kisses, warm cider, and warmer fires, chasing the cold away from their rooms and back out to sleep with Hope in the quiet, unforgiving night. They would sleep well until the morning, when they joyfully attended her death.

Oh, how they love watching witches die.

Even though visiting her could very well have brought the same fate to me, I had to try everything I could to break her free. Or I had to see her and kiss her one last time. From just off the road, hidden well in the dark, I watched for anyone coming 'round her, but no one did. My caution eventually gave way and I ran to my sister. She was cold and sick and wet with fever, her eyes barely there. She was already so close to death that I thought for a moment she wouldn't even make it through the night.

"Verity?" she'd whispered. Her voice was so quiet, hardly releasing words.

Minutes died with hurried conversation as we talked and wept.

The witching hour passed us.

I told her I loved her many times, and it felt so far from enough. I kissed her forehead and her cheeks. I eyed those damned iron hinges, thinking of any way to break her free from the wooden prison. We could still run away together, if only I could get her free. But even as I struggled to break her from the stocks, I realized it wouldn't matter. She was much too weak to flee anywhere.

She was so very far from me the whole time. Her eyes would fade and then slightly return, each time falling farther away from mine until the last little glint had all but disappeared.

I pressed my cheek to hers and waited for her to die.

Instead, when my face was down and I'd become lost in the slowing rhythm of her shallow breaths, she suddenly rose her moon-glowing eyes to mine and said her second last words.

Now I lie in bed, a failure in saving her, cursing the rising sun which sparkles through the window and into my tear-filled eyes. The same light will soon shine upon Hope's execution in a few hours.

But not just hers.

I clench my eyes shut, but in my mind, her words echo on.

***

I should have stepped out to a morning greyed by sadness. A morning as dark as my grieving heart. Leaving the house to attend an execution brings with it the belief that the land will mirror how I'm feeling inside—that the day would be as gloomy as I. But 'tisn't the case at all. The sky is blue as ever. The birds chirp cheerfully. Amidst this warm, cloudless afternoon, a knotted rope is slung over a beam, swaying ever so indifferently.

Goodmother has not yet said a word. She's right beside me and her eyes never meet mine. She is solemn as can be, pursed mouth, gritted teeth. Her hands clench the sides of her dress and even though she portrays every depth of her stoic nature, I can feel that she's all but a moment from falling apart.

We were forbidden from attending the trial and were told nothing of it. The guilty verdict only became known once we saw her being led through the village and to the stocks at dawn. Anyone that had been milling through the street had stopped to watch. In the goldening dark, many of Salem's people had left their homes to begin their morning errands and so most of the village bore witness to the convicted witch scuffing shamefully along the road. We all watched, but she never looked at us.

Walking with men at each arm, she seemed none worried 'tall. She appeared, rather, as if she was deep in thought, quietly walking to fetch some milk or to complete some other trivial task for the day. One of the men walking her had looked in our direction, catching eyes with most of the lingering watchers. They began to disperse and carry on their way at his stare, not wanting to draw any undue attention in the presence of a convicted witch. Suspected associations are enough to find one's self in trial.

I stayed anyway.

They took her up the platform steps and threw her body into the open, wooden mouth, slamming it shut over her back. Her knees struggled to find a resting place on the splintered boards as they latched the hinges. And then they left, leaving Hope confined in the street. 'Twas then she finally looked up. Her eyes found me and she spoke with them alone.

She told me to leave and I did as she asked.

A tense hand strikes my arm and squeezes hard, bringing me back from my thoughts. I look over and realize Goodmother has collected my arm as her own, but her eyes are fixed on the killing stage before us. The crowd hushes itself and over the spectators before me, I can just see the tops of heads walking in line toward the side of the platform. Ascending the stairs are two churchmen, followed by Hope and the elder from Grace's wedding. The men take their place at each side of her and the elder steps forward, addressing us all with serious eyes before speaking.

"Let me first say holy morning to us all. Though something as deplorable as death shall be granted to one today, it is but a necessary means – a removal of darkness to better allow the lord's light to cover our people. Meddling witches and any associations with dark arts or demonic play cannot be permitted to take root in our land, and if there are other heretics here today, hear me when I say you will be found out and you will be swiftly hung. For under the watchful eye of God, you cannot escape the lain fate of your trespasses."

Hope remains bowed of head, her hands tied in front of her, but in a natural way, as if they would be properly clasped just the same had they not been forced to do so.

"This whore'ish orphan whom stands before ye has no repentance for the actions of her unwedded sexual immorality. She was given a full examination by Doctor Coverdale, and a dutiful trial to expel the name of whoever is responsible for delivering her with child, and yet, she says there is none such man. The likely possibility then that the child is of a devilish origin must be considered and weighed against her lack of other confession. No name was ever given to us, though she was offered gracious opportunity, and so as it stands under the likelihood of dark consummation, Hope Bridgemaiden and her unborn shall be hung by the neck under God's sun until they are dead."

My body goes cold and my chest trembles. I feel tears warming the corners of my eyes and I clench my hands together in an effort to cease my shaking. I look around, anywhere other than the platform. My gaze falls from person to person, and the rage inside of me grows in witness of their somber indifference.

I spot Grace and her husband. She is staring at the ground and even as John coaxes her arm and whispers reassurances to her, it seems she has resolved herself to not lifting her eyes from their place. I wish she would. I wish she would notice me so we could comfort each other from afar. I keep my eyes on her for another moment, but to no avail.

"Step forward!"

My eyes shoot back to the platform where Hope has been led in front of the other people on stage. One man reaches and grabs for the noose above her, bringing it down to the front of her face. My stomach crashes and I feel I may throw up. She bows her head willfully and slips it through the rope, raising it again only when the rope is tightened. She looks at us all. Her eyes appear calm, hopeful... free. They seem to be looking far beyond us, toward the horizon or somewhere even further perhaps.

The elder halts the ropeman with a raised hand. He turns back toward Hope. "If you have final words or a name to confess who's brought child to you, speak now, witch. Speak or die."

Last night when I went to her, she would not even tell me who was responsible for the child inside her. I begged her to, but she said she couldn't and that I would never understand why, but that I had to trust her.

She brings her gaze back down to us, scanning the crowd over and making contact with as many individuals as she can. I feel so much love emanating from her, and not even the slightest bit of fear. "My people..." she extends her hands as if offering something to us, "I forgive you all."

The crowd shifts around me, discomforted by her lack of plea or cursings.

She continues, "Blindness plagues you, but you were made to be this way." She looks over to the elder. "Salem hides many secrets, for it is a town founded on deceit and sin, and witches have little to do with the true madness that prevails here, the madness that is levied upon our fragile minds when we are young. The madness of murder, control, and fear."

The elder motions to the ropeman with a panicky hand and the man readies himself for hanging.

Hope looks back to the crowd. She spots me. Our eyes lock and the most unbearable sadness I've ever felt crashes straight into my heart, nearly collapsing me. She smiles as if she hasn't seen me in a very long time and it keeps me standing.

"Truth does not come to you as a season," she continues, "it must be unearthed. It is buried and dirty, and hidden far away from you all. Do not be passive to the leaders. Do not be accepting to things if only out of tradition. And wheresoever you are told the monsters dwell, do not cower away, but go forth and discover them for yourselves. There is much to be learned from monsters."

"Silence, heathen!" The elder says, cutting her off. He turns to the ropeman once more. "Raise the witch."

Hope lays her hands gently upon her belly and looks down toward her unborn baby. She closes her eyes. "I'm so sorry, my love. Now we sleep together."

Before I can look away, the rope engages, pulling tight and raising her smoothly into the air. Her head stays forward facing; she doesn't slump, kick, or thrash. She appears to embrace her ascension. The rope stops lifting when she is but a few feet off the platform, and everyone holds their breath.

An eternity seems to pass yet no one makes a sound until her belly lain hands fall softly to her sides. I feel her leave me, and though I can barely contain the tears that pumping from my eyes by my heaving chest, I do feel a bit of gratitude buried under my sadness—gratitude that her death seemed so painless.

The crowd's collection of voices begin to rise as everyone starts shifting about, ready to leave and go about their day now that the theatrics of my sister's death are over. I glance up to her once more and I see a red ring hanging dead around her ankle.

The garter I'd given her has fallen.

My grief has become uncontrollable and my emotions erupt from me as I take off running away from the crowd. I run across the road in blind hysterics and into the woods. I run until no one can see me any longer and I collapse onto the ground, the most broken and helpless I've ever been.

ONE YEAR LATER

CHAPTER THREE

I never wanted to be here. Fearful breaths pulsate from beneath his frail bones. The harvest moon's light cuts through the black and illuminates the trembling creature in my hand, turning his wide obsidian eyes into glassy screams from which I hear all the terror he shall not ever speak.

Behind the orphanage, I stand alone for the first time in my life with execution orders in my mind and a heartily worn knife in my grip, handed to me by Goodmother to carry out murder in the name of a stew dinner.

I look down at him, his tiny body quivering between my clenched fingers and he stares back as if to silently plead the question: *why are you doing this to me?* Those eyes hold life behind them like little windows – two small panes housing something eternal and innocent which looks outward only to see this terrible world and all the darkness it has.

For close to an hour now I have stood at the killing stump, barefoot, freezing, and unable to do anything but look at the dried blood stains which run down every side of it. Black patterned shadows of death cover most of the rippled wood in the darkness which has descended upon the village and I stand here trapped inside my own conscience.

The air has become so much colder tonight. Protective tears seep into my eyes with each passing breeze and my cheeks tingle as it sweeps my shielding hair back, exposing my face fully to its chill. The dewed grass below my feet has stiffened into little icy claws, rising out of the ground as if from a legion of frost demons whom dwell below the earth. Scraping for my flesh, they inject their cold into my toes and it rises up swiftly through my blood and deep into my bones. Yet I remain here, trying desperately to put off the inevitable horror in which I must forcibly partake.

The rabbit squeals softly with the slightest plea for pardon and my heart breaks.

It isn't as if I haven't ever eaten rabbit before; I have many times. It was always my sisters who did the butchering, sparing me of any role in the killing part. They're all gone now, leaving me to be the sole girl residing at Bridge To Salvation Orphanage.

Or rather "Bridge To Hell" as I prefer to call it.

Examining the rabbit's neck, I brush his bristled fur back, searching for any sign of an artery. I believe if his blood were to pour out quickly, his pain would pass just the same. I haven't an idea whether that is true, but I need at least one comforting thought in this nightmarish situation. Nothing seems to quell the thought of murder from making me ill and sad. Surely I can say that being a ministry raised Puritan girl and as well versed in scripture as I am, I know there is nothing at all written in that book about the execution of defenseless woodland animals.

Where would it leave my soul?

My mind settles on the word and tries to touch it – *soul* – and through the grasp of my wonder it slips away like vapor and leaves only emptiness behind. I'm quite doubtful of most everything that holds prominence in this village. Often I think of heaven and I try to envision the most extraordinary paradise where everything glints of gold, but my thoughts never stay there for long. They always descend immediately to Hell, leaving me to tremble under the torture of my own imagination. Most sadly it seems, the more I attempt to make any sense of such things, the more lost I become. As of late I doubt most everything, especially heaven.

Shivering and twirling the knife between my frozen fingers, I am iced by indecision. I look up to the dusky sky above. How starry and still it all is behind my quick condensing breaths. My lips blow them out as if they are pieces of my soul longing to kiss the sky. I watch them dissipate up into the brightened night, toward the mysterious moon which sits just over the wooded tree line.

Lost in the celestial world above, my eye catches a flickering of orange glow atop the grass to my right. I snap my gaze over to the source and I see a hulking shadow blocking a good portion of the back door entry, allowing only a thin frame of firelight to escape.

Standing in the doorway is Goodmother, and she looks hellishly displeased.

"Bridgemaiden, must you take so long? It has grown dark and instead of partaking in this meal you may well become one, now finish with haste and bring it here!"

"Pardon me a few more minutes," I reply.

She crosses her arms in front of her with an air of command. "I won't have that wandering nighttime beast claiming the last of my children."

Even from where I stand, I can see but the slightest bit of embarrassment come over her face in response to the compassion that has just slipped her tongue.

"Wh-what I mean to say is… if you were to be killed and eaten, it would reflect very poorly on my ability to care for the church's children and they would not be forgiving with me one bit!" She slams the door shut, leaving me in the cold, quiet darkness once again.

I turn back toward the stump, looking past it to the darkened, eerie woods just beyond. "Oh, but I thought God watches over us all?" I say aloud to no one as I try to focus my sight as deep into the forest as possible. Everything back there remains nothing but a swirling black soup; a world lost within that could only be explored by one willing to die in there.

I feel so attracted to the woods. So drawn to the mystery. To the danger of what could be within.

Ever since Hope and I found the peculiar deer body, there have been many gruesome occurrences of livestock slain in the night, discovered by the owning villagers the following morning. The more sensible folk believe it to be a mad wolf, left without a pack and probably starving. The odd thing about these attacks however, is the condition of each animal's remains: the same as the doe. Only the blood was drained, the flesh left as it was. This of course leads to the more reaching rumors of demonic presences, witches' sorcery, and even some rumblings that the dark lord Satan himself walks these grounds.

Some nights I sit at my window long into the twilight of the early mornings and I watch and wait, hoping to catch a glimpse of the one who prowls our village. I have yet to see anything clear, but once in a while, I swear I see a silhouette just at the edge of the trees where the blackness bleeds into complete dark.

Still holding the rabbit and without much time left to decide his fate, I choose against my proper judgment to simply let him go. I bend over, setting the trembling creature down on the ground and it springs instantly back to life, rocketing off into the night with swift and silent leaps toward the trees.

I turn around to head inside the house, knowing full well of the tongue lashing I'm about to receive, when I feel it.

Back bared to the woods, I know it's there. It's watching me.

I hear a squeal barely join the still air—the same squeal I heard from the rabbit earlier. Then a brief rustle from within the forest. Then nothing.

Nothing but a feeling – a chill that rises through me and around my shoulders, up the sides of my neck and into my body. I can feel its power radiating from beyond the shadows, creating an inferiority one would feel while in the presence of a beast much greater than themselves. Not like a bear though...

This feels different.

I can feel it thinking, holding itself back from attacking, even vulnerable as I stand.

Take a step, I tell myself. *Move.*

Walking with hasty strides toward the orphanage's back door, I resist the growing urge to run fed by the immeasurable fear rising within me. I reach the door quickly (as it was not but twenty paces away) but before I burst through safely into the light and warmth inside, a thought comes over me.

If it wanted to kill me just now, it would have. So why am I afraid?

I turn around and face the woods once more. After a moment and before thinking, I speak out into the night. "I do not fear you as the others do!"

A moment passes and I am not graced with a reply.

"Perhaps I shall come out to see you one night if you should grant it?"

Not a rustle, not a twig crunch, no sound at all.

After a disappointed pause, I turn back toward the door to enter the house. I place my hand on the frigid iron doorknob and I get the most unexplained feeling from the woods at my back, like a silent agreement that slides into my body. Strangely enough, this excites me, for it is quite risky to be proposing oneself to things so dangerously unknown.

And yet, I am too tired of this life to stay away.

***

Goodmother is quite a scary person when she's mad. A solid woman she is, with wispy graying hair and a frame which has acquired the thickness of an ornery old swine. Her stature is unkindly layered like stone slabs as opposed to the soft, billowy fat of most women her age. Intimidating to say the least, she is seldom the person I should ever want to admit my shortcomings to.

As I step out of the cold night and into the warm house, I shoulder the heavy wooden door closed then lock it, silently preparing for nothing but the worst.

THWACK!

My humble entry is shattered as she slams a heavy knife down through a cabbage and into the maple table with far more force than required to chop the vegetable. I can see her wrinkled brow of disdain accentuated by the roaring stove fire set for supper. I decide it best to speak first, if only I may be delivered from this lingering tension.

"My apologies, Goodmother," I say. "The haste of the rabbit greatly surprised me as he kicked and kicked some more until he fell from my grip and ran off into the night."

I hold my breath, laden with guilt, not sure if she believes my lie. As I slip my stockings back on, I contemplate whether or not to offer any more explanation when she abruptly speaks.

"'Tis the gratitude I receive, child?" she says. "Indecent respect for my kindness in suggesting we share a pleasant evening meal absent of bread or milk? Well then, I will eat this game-less cabbage stew and you shall eat nothing." She groans, scooping the scattered vegetables into her apron which she had formed into a sort of basket-like bowl of cloth.

I suddenly realize I haven't a care, for somehow even her anger seems meaningless as my thoughts remain only with the woods and whatever dwells within them.

"Study the good scripture for tomorrow, Book of Job. It had better be sound enough for judgment," she says, tossing the vegetables into a boiling pot hanging over the flames.

"I let the rabbit go," I slip out in quick defiance, betraying myself as I turn and begin to walk toward the scripture room.

She stops moving for a moment, then after a pause, resumes preparing for dinner. She says nothing in reply.

I turn back to face her so as not to show cowardice. "I suppose I want to be known for the truth, even if it upsets you to hear it."

"Be gone now," she says. "Show your worth and find redemption in the word, for I sense from you displeasing thoughts as of late."

I sigh. "Thanks be unto you," I say (the standard valediction) quite sarcastically as I exit the fire-lit kitchen. I make way into the darkened study room, moving toward the far wall where the sitting table rests on the cold, plank-cracked floor. I slink myself across the bench and into the dark shadows of the corner in which I so often spend time losing myself to lavish daydreams. For myself, dreams are most easy to come by in this horridly dreary life. Much easier than "faith" is anyway.

This corner of the house hides no flaws, mind you. The rest of the structure is sound enough, adorned more so than a typical colonial house and quite roomy with four bedrooms and a loft. It is the foundation however that remains the true problem. It had not been erected correctly and is set on poorly graded land with drooping, bowed, and splintering logs meeting at the corner of the southernmost side. This remains the only spot to suffer from the weak under-structure.

'Tis where the house bible sits, lain open across the slanted table, sliding farther down each day until someone pulls it from the daunting edge and rights it again to its central place.

Reading the passages and parables every day was most unpleasant as I thought them to be nothing worthy of my favor. I grow quite sad now though, for I desperately miss the company of my sisters as we read together in our shared misery. The house now so quiet without them.

I deplore my life and sometimes I wish I would go to sleep and never wake up. Perhaps I could open my window on the night of a dead, cold December and go to sleep forever, letting the wintry breath come in and guide me away. I wasn't always this sad, but it seems all that brings me happiness is gone or forbidden.

I wish for few things – simple things. I wish for freedom. I wish to speak of my mind. I wish to not hide my eyes from wandering. I wish to know who my mother is. I wish I could be free to believe in whatever I feel to be true to myself. I wish to scream as I please, to run away, to live fearlessly.

Mostly, I wish to seek truth—to find it. To find love.

Are these not desired by everyone?

Some seem to risk death for it, so I suppose they are. 'Tis been one year today since my sister Hope was sentenced to death for becoming with child with a man whom she had not married. A man who no one knows.

I see her still, swaying slowly like a pendulum in the sky. Just a corpse with hands fallen from her baby's tomb.

Tears form warm in my eyes and I try to push it all away, but my heart shakes.

Such horrible things as death and sickness, burials and hangings seem to plague my life now as I approach womanhood. My innocence has since been turned to ash with those of the supposed witches I have seen burned on their kindled mounds. God, who is so readily spoken of during these events, must be sorrowfully displeased by such darkness within our community.

I pull a match from a box at the corner of the table and light the study candle, sending a small flame to flicker its light excitedly around the room. I open the book to somewhere in the middle. My eyes settle on an open page before me, but I do not see words. My focus broadens and all I see are indistinguishable lines of ink on paper. These lines which are responsible for so many punishments. For Hope and her baby's death. I wish I were on any of those first boats to the colonies. I would've thrown every one of these books into the ocean and watched the papers of men become eaten by the sea.

Life would be better and my sister would be here to share it with me.

I close the book, fold my hands to my elbows, and start to sob into the dark hollow my arms have made, tears dripping off my face and onto the oak table. I cry for a long time—the longest since her death.

A time passes. The light flickers still on the other side of my eyelids.

My crying slows, and the only tears left have dampened my eyelashes, but no more come. I feel my body begin to calm. There is space in my breaths now and between those spaces, the same words fit into them like a coffin in the ground, waiting to be covered by the earth, buried as a memory.

I miss you, Hope.

***

I lift my head and look around the room, but nothing can be seen.

The candle! It must have gone out. I reach over and touch where it stands and feel only a small mound of cold wax encircling the base. How long have I been asleep? Hours at least. Goodmother would be furious if she knew. Sunday mornings she always discusses the assigned passages with me before I leave for service and if she finds out I did not complete my studying, she'll surely lash me a good bit.

I'll take the book up to my room and study quick. The moonlight is always bright in Salem and sits in the frame of my window's view in the hours of early morning.

I gather the heavy block of scripture, careful not to drop it for a book that size would likely wake the village. Precariously, I cradle it to my chest, fighting the sleepiness which still moves like syrup into my eyelids as I make my way to the staircase. In most houses, the wood which stairs are built of is quite creaky, making it impossible to sneak anywhere. Here however, I believe that all the running my sisters and I did up and down them has worn them solidly quiet. We had much fun stomping all of the creaks away.

Keeping my steps light anyway, I am relieved when no groans or bends alert the old witch of my curfew breach. Reaching the top, I move quickly like a ghost down the hallway and right into my bedroom, closing the door, but not all the way for the latch is the only loud part of it.

Even the floorboards of my room creak not one bit as I move toward my bed.

Perfect silence.

I slip my bonnet off in one motion, not even bothering to untie it. My hair falls out of it and around my face and I leave it to tickle my cheeks because it feels like freedom. I undo my petticoat and let it fall to the floor, then I drop my gown, stepping out of it like a puddle. I remove my wool stockings and am reminded of how stark-cold the wood is under my feet. Lastly, I pull my shift up over my head and throw it to the side.

For a few moments in the night, I am free.

I move nakedly through my room, spinning with arms out and head back, my skin tightening all over in the frigid air. A few minutes pass of gliding and smiling and I am soon standing in front of my window, marveling at my reflection.

The forest outside shows through my figure in the glass as if I am a ghost, transparent in the moonlight but not absent of details. I look into my own eyes for a moment. They seem older. My skin, always pale, is powdery in the lunar light. I hold my breasts and give them a slight squeeze. Small and firm and virginal they are, but still like a child's to me. I wish I were older and fuller and prettier. I want to be a woman now, so I may leave. Maybe I'll go back to England and travel a world away from here. Maybe I'll go somewhere more exotic where life is a foreign paradise of sunshine and color and swirling flutes singing about the air in beautiful markets.

I just want to be gone from here.

I move from the window and into bed with the cumbersome old book. Lessons, lessons, lessons – all so stupid and boring. I've forgotten what my assigned one is, so instead I turn to the pages I always covet on cold nights like these when I lay restless and naked with my unquieted mind. Lost in the metaphors, I find my own pleasure, for I believe there is no such wrong in doing so. I begin to read, my pulse rising as the words fly by my eyes. They devour them eagerly as I begin my usual ritual.

I have taken off my robe –

My beloved thrust his hand in through the latch opening –

In the darkness, far from Goodmother's detection and with calculated routine, I slip my hand with practiced stealth under the blankets, then onto my warm skin. I pause, then a bit further. I close my eyes, running Solomon's song through my mind.

Her hands dripped with myrrh –

Dripping on the handles of her lock –

I begin to dance my fingertips around, soft at first, then a bit quicker, keeping the rhythm steady…

My thoughts drift to an old town proverb I have heard more frequently than I care to say:

"Idle hands are the Devil's workshop."

Since mine are quite busy, I must be doing God's work after all.

The song, burned into my mind, continues.

And at my gate is all manner of pleasant fruit –

Shallow breaths escape my lips, quicker and quicker as my lusting inside tightens. I escalate now, close to the summit, trembling in truth, so rightfully lost in my own paradise I am.

Then blinding white bells come raging in and I go dark and starry all at once.

***

A pain cracks through my face like I have never felt before, my secret pleasure shattered by a strike delivered out of the darkness and into the side of my head so hard it must've come from none other than God himself.

I open my eyes and white stars hover in front of everything. My wrist is grabbed and I'm lifted, slamming my knee into a bedpost as I'm ruggedly dragged out from under the blankets and tossed into the corner onto the frigid wooden floor.

"Shall be no such things in this house!" Goodmother growls, looming over me in such a way I feel much smaller than I already am.

As my brain begins to come back to a sensible place, I realize that she must have seen me from the doorway, for it hadn't been latched shut. She was always catching us girls in our wrongdoings, but I had always been so careful with *this*, for I knew of the retribution awaiting me if I were to be caught.

"I shall do as I please for I am not a child!" I scream carelessly before my thoughts can fully clear.

"Well then," she replies, "I shall also do as *I* please—that should be just, granted by your laws of course. Now stand up."

"No." The word tastes like sugar.

She reaches down, grabbing my wrist again, and I resist with every ounce of strength I have, which is little opposition against her livestock corralling arms. She stands me up and even though I had made my legs limp, somehow they find form again beneath me. She grips my small curled fingers inside her massive fist. "Shall I break these now?"

"Do as you wish," I reply. "I've already memorized what I want. I have no need to turn any pages in that stupid book again."

She holds my hand with quivering tension grinding the bones of my knuckles together with the cold, inhuman disregard that only an old Puritan wench like her could possess. "If you shan't any longer have the ability to do actions against yourself like a devilish animal, I have no regret in turning the pages of the good book for you."

"And I haven't a problem finding any man to do my devilish actions for me!" I snap back. "For even broken, I'm far less repulsive than yourself!"

She hits me across the face again. This time real tears form and fall. She has let go of me and step back and I turn to face her, my chest heaving and lip quivering, trying so hard not to cry.

But then it all explodes.

"Go on, break me then! Beat this little orphan girl you hate so much and leave me for dead like you did Hope. What can you do to me? I'm not scared of you. Kill me. I don't care!" The shouted words break through cries and her face falls somber as I move toward her fearlessly.

She doesn't back up and before I know it, I fall into her arms, wrapped in the comfort of embrace but still with a heavy, lonely, desperate wish to be free of here one way or another. I cry for a long while, and even in her hug, I still feel far away.

"Go on now and cover yourself, Verity so we can talk," she says.

I separate from her and move toward the bed, grabbing the hefty blanket up and tossing it around myself like an enormous robe, and then I sit down, lips and legs still trembling.

"Speak whatever is on your mind child," she says with a long sigh. "I will listen with God here and now and together we will solve whatever it is that troubles you."

"I'm not speaking to God," I reply.

"Fine then," she says with eyes wanting to say so much more. "Tell me what it is that bothers you so."

"Everything bothers me. My life is nothing but sadness and secrets," I reply, looking out the window across the room from us.

"What is it you mean?"

"What good is there in my life? I have no purpose," I reply. "Chores, scripture, and my mind are all I have. This village feels like a prison of routine and sin and I feel like a criminal every day. I feel like my thoughts are patrolled and that they must be hidden all the time from everyone. I question so much Goodmother and I feel so alone with all the weight that's always on my mind. It leaves me so sad and weak and it makes me care about nothing. Sometimes at night, feeling my skin, my naked self – it's an escape for me. It is but a few moments I ever have that make me feel wonderful and beautiful and *alive*."

A moment of silence passes between us and she shifts about, presumably figuring how best to handle all of my words.

"Only Hope understood," I say softly.

"What happened to Hope was her fault alone, Verity. She knew the laws here."

"Death should never be a sentence for something as wonderful as becoming with child."

"She did so out of wedlock."

"So she dies for that?" I say. "And what of the baby? That's her charge as well?"

"Yes."

"You are just as bad as them, Goodmother," I reply. "You helped murder them both and I hate you for it. I will hate you always for it."

"Feel as you will," she says. "I didn't make her decisions."

"I believe you'd feel differently had it been you with a rope around your neck," I reply. "But instead you just raise orphans you don't like, tell them nothing of their past, and look away when they are hung."

"I don't know of your past, Verity."

"Ask God. I'm sure he knows and yet will say nothing to you about it."

"Verity, I know your life is hard and you have no sisters at the orphanage to share in anything with. I'm sorry you know not who your parents are and that you question God, laws, scripture, and life. It will always be hard for you this way. But you must think of your future, of marriage and children and what will happen to your soul should you die. I only want what's best for you, child. Align yourself with God and with Salem. Now try and sleep well and be ready for service in the morning. Try to find some joy in it all. You cannot fight this life forever."

I say nothing and make it quite clear that I am done talking. She rises slowly and moves out of the room without saying anything more. I fall onto my side and begin to weakly slip into sleep with a soul now empty of ache and hollow tears lingering on my cheeks. Wrapped up in the warm blankets, I fall lucidly away without the slightest bit of hope for anything more than my sentence of a bleak and worthless life.

There is no forever.

CHAPTER FOUR

I step outside and the chill of the misty morning slaps my face like a slab of ice. The greeting provides an uncomfortable welcome as I start my trip toward the worst event of every week: Sunday morning service.

When the winter shivers find our bones, we can always cover with more clothes to slow the creep of cold, but in that chapel, nothing can be added to protect one's soul from the feeling of nakedness endured under the heavy charges of sin. No villager here is free of trespasses. Wild accusations regularly leave the lips of Salem's locals, at most times hardly anything more than gossip, yet these half-truths seem to make their way about with arbitrary madness just the same. Everyone believes everything to be true when it is gossiped about.

Everything that encompasses Salem's church I find detestable, but what I despise the most is that 'tis mandatory to attend. I never pay much attention to what is said, but after years of scripture lessons, I do know that imposing religiousness was against what Jesus had taught. He never forced anyone to follow him, and so it seems quite a contradiction then that this rigidity had ever been allowed to take root in a country colonized by those seeking religious freedom.

But there is no freedom in this life. I am nothing more than a young orphan girl with orders to abide by. Orders that require me to attend a service where judgment, prejudice, accusations, gossip, and sin are the only subjects spoken of.

How could God ever be found in such a terrible place?

Upon opening the door, I keep my gaze low and walk hurriedly with hands clasped in front of myself, always waist high, like a proper woman. I enter the area of congregation and shuffle myself into a pew next to another somber faced girl, perhaps a few years older than I. We exchange the briefest of smiles and then affix our eyes back up to the front at the sound of the heavy side door being opened then slammed shut.

Minister Barrowe enters the room with a swift, burly energy, his thick soled boots booming with each step as the lingering whispers die to nothing. He is a tall, husky man with a large head topped with peppered brown and grey hair neatly combed back and a face full of big, expressive features that could easily convey his mood even to the townsfolk sitting in the farthest back corners of the chapel.

He approaches the podium at the front of the room, and everyone holds their breath in anticipation of what he will say today. He walks by, his eyes scan the congregation like a wolf searching for prey, and the look of displeasure on his face begins to make everyone uneasy.

"Today we shall not waste any time, but instead shall address this growing fear of evil among us," he says with his customary conviction. "I say there is a demon lurking that seems to think we are a weak and fearful bunch from a foreign land – unfamiliar with this new territory and afraid to expand into the unknown world beyond." Throwing his arm out in point toward the window over his head framing the rising sun, he narrows his eyes. "I say to thee, and you shall agree that we as Puritans have our faith for all eternity!"

The congregation begins to nod in somber unison, obeying the will of this man. Proclaiming voices rise as well in anxious but hushed conversations.

I pull at the loose, fraying strings of my dress, sending them into the air and watching as they flutter to the floor. My doubts become stirred on these mornings and my questions of faith become so loud, sometimes I panic for a moment and I almost think those around me can hear the disbeliefs being shouted from my mind.

"What do you think of this demon or creature?"

Over the minister's large but droning voice, I'm surprised by a soft female tone coming from the girl sitting to my left. Her head had not turned and her eyes had not wavered from the minister's place, but she spoke to me.

No one ever speaks to me.

I take a quick moment to decide upon a response – to decide whether I can speak my mind to her, and yet my mouth opens before I can stop myself. "I believe that Satan would not care so much as to come reside outside of Salem Village, as our colony is quite small and quite boring."

I hadn't noticed fully how beautiful this girl is when I spoke, but now as I stare into her strikingly large blue eyes waiting for her response, my gaze travels along her golden locks that fall rebelliously from the sides of her bonnet which covers a radiant mane trapped underneath the white, formally dry headpiece. She almost sparkles against the drab backdrop of the meetinghouse.

"So a wolf then?"

"Possibly," I reply, pausing as I feel a smirk creep across my lips. "Or perhaps maybe 'tis the minister himself?"

The girl's eyebrows arch in surprise. "Surely not – for why would he do something like that? Quite senseless it would be."

"I'm merely remarking on the similarities, for he is big, hairy, and scary as well," I reply, giggling under my breath.

She leans in a bit closer. "Very funny, but hardly believable I should think."

"Believable? So you believe then that a demonic being wandering about our village foraging on livestock blood is more likely than a crazy minister with a knife?"

"I didn't say that."

"Well I hope there's a demon after all," I say with a sigh. "Such a thing could transform this dreary life into quite an exciting one."

"Or a darkened one," she whispers.

I wish I could tell her all of my thoughts. I feel so compelled to share them sometimes. I wish I could tell her of my tempting the alleged demon of the woods the night before, of how I wish to join it or run away into the uncertain forest alone, to die or find some life other than this one. Alas, I cannot, for we are here and that could be dangerous. I suppose it doesn't matter anyway; in two hours when service concludes,

I will be tending once again to all of the boring household chores that make up my life – sweeping, cooking, collecting firewood, tending linens, making candles, studying scripture and lastly, off to bed only to awaken at dawn and repeat this forced routine day after day after day until I get married off to some horrible man like my other sisters. Even then, the chores will continue.

This girl beside me though, she is such a beautiful interruption to what would otherwise be a dreadful day, and I am grateful for her company.

The low hum of grouped voices becomes suddenly louder, pulling me out of my drifting thoughts, and as they do, the minister's ranting voice comes back to me.

"– and this demon is going to persist with terrorism of our people until he is eliminated from the land! This expelling will require great resolve as well as a great hunt from the good men of Salem village! Any suspicious behavior is the work of heresy until proven otherwise by myself and the elder counsel and must be reported as such with ruthless consequence for withholding or concealing the practicing work of Satan."

"Witches!" yells a male churchgoer. The rustle of shifting bottoms against mahogany benches accompany an air of uneasy whispering amongst the people. The minister straightens up and seems to radiate an energy immediately fed by this shouted comment; as if he was hoping this subject would arise.

"Witches you say?" His large dense hands slam onto the sides of the podium. "Indeed this is of rightful contemplation, is it not? These witches are certainly present, perhaps even among us now?" He steps from behind the podium and begins to pace in even strides before the seated people.

"Do you believe in witches?" I ask the girl.

"I am not sure," she replies, "but I fear we should listen to what he has to say on them."

I ignore her diversion. "My sisters told me that if you pull a hair from the head of a witch and hold it up to the light of a full moon, it will glow."

"I think if there was truth to that, the minister would have brought all the villagers out into the night to have this done."

"I don't believe so," I say. "It would be weak for a man of God to demonstrate a faith in magic."

Her eyes still ahead, I see her smirk from the corner of her mouth. "Let us listen now."

I bring my attention back up to the bellowing minister, but not before I take one more long look at her.

"When these talks arise, the maddened become fearful of being found, and I can tell you with great certainty that these witches – should they be present here or elsewhere – will hide their true nature well from us." He turns slowly to his left and locks eyes with a bench of young unwed women. "In regard to the rumors of unholy consummation that I have been hearing as of late, it seems as if the witches are growing either in numbers, or their encounters in prevalence; either way, cunning these women are and vigilant you men must be."

I turn to flash the girl a smile, and I know she feels my eyes on her because she looks to me as well. Even though she's a bit older than I, she blushes at the minister's implications.

"Have you ever been in the undressed company of a man

before?" I ask as quietly and politely as possible.

"I do not fancy a man. Not one bit," the girl replies, her face turning quite serious. "I know not what you likely think, but I find the idea of lying with one quite appalling."

"They do smell like pigs, I suppose."

We giggle too loudly and a stern usher appears behind us, poking our shoulder blades with a sharp jab from a wooden staff, presumably to remind us of appropriate service conduct. He then turns and marches as a soldier would toward the other side of the meetinghouse.

"I would like a man. Not for marriage, just to see what it is like," I say.

"And risk death?" the girl replies.

"We risk death every day in this horrible colony, do we not?"

"Life is dangerous indeed, but we shan't seek it out."

"It is not death I seek, but life – real living, free and far away from... *this*."I say, looking around with disgust. "You should know, I am not afraid to take risks."

The girl looks forward again. "Neither am I, for I am married."

I snap my head to look at her, surprised by the comment. She hardly gives the impression of a woman under union.

"But you said –"

"I know what I said," she cuts my words short. "But marriage and desire are rarely the same. My husband and I –" she stops. "Never mind."

I debate for a moment what next to say, then without thinking I blurt out, "You are foolish."

"I'm foolish! And how so exactly?"

"I don't know – I'm sorry," I respond, ashamed of my outburst. "I shouldn't judge you for making a life that brings you happiness." I feel the slightest twinge of jealousy rise inside my heart as I pretend to look back up toward the minister.

"I'm not happy," she replies. "I hate my life."

"Why did you choose to marry then?"

"Some things are chosen for us. Sometimes life is simply beyond our control."

"I don't believe that. I believe we choose our own destiny."

She forces a smile. "Someday you shall see how untrue that really is."

Rather than argue with her any more, I simply take a brief silence and fidget in my pew, aware of how uncomfortable I am. I avert my eyes from the girl and scan the sea of indistinguishably morose faces on those who have handed their life over to this church; this Puritanical way of existence. A feeling comes over me – a feeling that perhaps the girl is right.

Maybe a dreary life is a fate for all – even myself – for how could I ever stop it?

I look back at the girl. knowing service will be concluded soon and fearing to end our acquaintance in bitterness, I decide to speak to her once more.

"I did not mean for my words to get away from me," I say softly. "'Tisn't my place to judge you, for I despise those who do it to me."

She side-eyes me and bows her head slightly as if to say: *you are forgiven.*

"I know we have spoken only a short while, but I feel as if we could be –"

"Never mind this talk," she says sharply. "I shall not speak of my life in this place any longer, and certainly not to you. I've already said too much."

In an unexpected instant, her cold dismissal of my company banishes what hope I had for perhaps making a new friend.

Hurt, I look away, trying to hide my sadness.

The somber faces hardly reflect the joy that is constantly praised yet never seen. The room is packed full of those who follow a doctrine, older ones wrinkled and weathered from this life, the young ones eager to gain more, all seeking comfort within God's will as spoken to them from the minister. With a vision differing so much from the others, alone I shall always be if I cannot find a friend. While I can't be sure, a strange inkling remains that this girl feels the same as I. However more reserved in her ways, I suspect she is afraid.

"I haven't even a single friend in this colony," I whisper. "My parents are gone and I am an orphan under this horrible church. I am sorry if I offended you, but I feel as if we could be –"

"It isn't you. I speak of nothing on that subject if only for fear of what could be done to me if I did. That is all."

We fall silent together and continue listening to the minister's sermon. However, quiet restlessness lingers – an unexplained closeness between us. There's an attraction I feel to her that I cannot ignore, and I believe she feels it too.

The minister continues, "It needs not be said that there have been speakings of men lying with men, and women lying with women, even in wedded homes."

Women lying with women? The thought slices through my mind like a curious knife.

Do such things occur?

I look back toward the girl, and with those ideas still swirling inside my mind, I catch myself admiring her lips, then with a bit of hesitation I give my eyes permission to fall onto her breasts, perhaps to prove myself wrong...

"To spare the children, and the rest of us from listening to such a disturbing discussion, I will just briefly state that it is of my personal opinion, as well as the counsel's, that any villager found to be engaging in such insultingly despicable acts will be promptly hung without possibility for pardon."

The girl's serene face shifts into a look of covered, but intense fear at the minister's words, eyes lighting up as if the minister himself had accused her specifically. She raises her shaking hands in a praying motion, then sets them clenched together back into her lap, quivering from her restless legs, bouncing at a nervous pace all the while.

Then, turning with desperate fear in her eyes, she looks deep into mine.

I feel her truth. And for her sake, I hope I'm the only one.

"I know what you cannot say," I whisper, slipping my hand steadily across her lap and into her hand. I intertwine my fingers with hers, our cold sweaty palms warming into one. "Please, do not be afraid."

The girl's face flushes red as she grips my hand with trembling tension; growing stronger by the moment.

Then she suddenly pulls away.

"Not here," she says. "We cannot talk of such things."

"I know," I reply. "What is your name?"

"Purity – Purity Lightfoot."

"I am Verity Bridgemaiden. When shall we be able to talk more?"

"I do not know," she responds. "They are quite condemning of talk such as ours."

"I do not condemn them though," I say. "For it is their way – a way in which we must all live if we are to make it in this life."

She grabs my hand once more. "I condemn them all and you should do the same, if only silently in your heart."

***

Service concludes abruptly, startling my drifting attention back to the moment. After some final speakings, all of the congregation members rise and make their way in uniform politeness toward the large doors, engaging in loud conversation full of hearty laughs and fake entangling small talk.

Purity and I rise as well, but before we can engage in any more personal conversation, our company is interrupted by a tall, thin, skeleton-like man with an ill-fitting suit and dark eyes who appears beside us in startlingly quiet fashion. It takes me a moment to recognize him. He's the elder who married Grace and murdered Hope. I shudder and take a step away from him.

"Who here is Verity Bridgemaiden?"

"I, sir."

"Ah – good then," he replies. "I am Elder Vines. I have a message for you."

My skin crawls and I restrain a glare with all my will.

I know who you are.

"A message?" I say.

"Yes. You are to make your exit and wait for the minister behind the meetinghouse. He is to meet you there in a moment."

"What for?"

"The reason matters not," he says sternly. "You best leave your questions in your head, child. Perhaps he will address such a thing with you."

He smiles another creepy grin full of thin lips and rotting teeth. His eyes say that he knows exactly what the meeting is about, but he enjoys keeping it from me anyway. He then turns and makes his way back into the crowd where his slinky frame disappears.

Purity and I begin making our way toward the doors, pushing ourselves behind the remaining ones who lag behind for the great warmth that the church stoves provide.

"You should go now. This is worrisome," Purity says.

"Worry not," I say, rolling my eyes. "The minister is a serious man, but not with regard to a wretched orphan like myself."

"Well, you must go nonetheless, but perhaps we shall meet later? I can watch for you to go to the watering stream near the cave bluffs."

"And I shall tell you of this senseless meeting."

"Yes. Now go. Do not leave him waiting."

"I will meet you just before nightfall. Bid me luck!"

We step outside into the frigid air and blinding sunshine. Purity turns and makes quick, graceful work of the meetinghouse steps before heading down the road. I watch her for a minute through squinted eyes, admiring the way her hips sway. Her shape is quite noticeable even beneath the unflattering garments with which they are covered. I hope I fill out the same way, though destined to remain small and frail forever is what I believe is closer to the truth.

I begin to make my way around the side of the meetinghouse, when before I can even arrive at the destination, a hulking shadow appears beside me. 'Tis Minister Barrowe.

"Verity Bridgemaiden?"

"Indeed, sir," I reply, curtsying as respectfully as possible. "Greetings to you this holy morning."

"We shall take a walk together outside if that'd be alright, for it is a cold but beautiful day," he says, removing his giant coat and placing it around my shoulders. "I have some matters that I would like to discuss but briefly with you."

We begin walking down the road away from the hustle and bustle of central morning activity and toward the other edge of the village which I have rarely seen. This is the side of the town which leads onto a main road, sending one toward other towns such as those of the Quakers and the Deutsche. I know barely anything of these people, but I know they are out there, and that gives me a dim hope I suppose.

"What are your years?" he asks.

"Fifteen, sir."

"And are you fed well? You look but twelve."

"Yes, sir."

"I pay for your meals, you know. I shall pay more if you are hungry."

"No, sir. I am cared for quite well, there is no need."

"So your Goodmother – she is diligent to your needs then, and fair would you say?"

"I suppose, yes."

"She seems to be quite concerned of you it seems."

"What of?"

"Your faith – among other things," he says, stopping to square up with me. "I shall be fully honest with you Verity, if you shall do the same."

"Of course, sir."

He continues leading me once again, nodding to a group of passerby who seem very interested in the fact that he is accompanied by me. As they pass, the minister tips his hat toward them. Then I notice, out of the group of mostly women, 'tis the young man who tips his hat back in the same customary gesture that a fellow would display toward a woman he fancies.

"What are the matters that trouble you, sir?" I ask.

He looks down at me then forward again, staring somberly into the distance. "She spoke of a quarrel between you two," he says, rubbing his beard. "One in which you shouted in great resentment of your Puritan life, or perhaps just of God maybe?"

I stare at the ground, fearful of what would become of me if I spoke in truth.

"Whatever is on your mind, say it, child," he says with a hint of commandment. "I may be a minister, but even I myself have questions from time to time. That is part of faith. What is it that troubles you?"

"Everything, sir," I reply, looking up at him. "My existence seems worthless sometimes, for I have nothing but questions – never contentment."

"There are times in which we all do, but you gain no enjoyment from your life?"

"I do in my dreams."

"You find none in the scripture?" he says with a sigh.

"I seek it, but I find only confusion instead. Confusion and old words written by old men a very long time ago."

"Your Goodmother tells me differently – she says you did indeed find pleasure in the word. Most *inappropriately* it seems."

I turn my eyes toward the ground in grave embarrassment.

"'Tis quite alright, dear. I forgive you," he says, tilting my chin upward. "You are a young woman now, with needs and desires in which you cannot find rest from. We all have them. I am afraid to say it, but such is the truth. It is how we rise above this desire that is of most importance."

"Sir, I will not have any such desires from thence on."

"That is impossible without prayer. We must be praying on such things. Use the scriptures in appropriate fashion to rid yourself of such feelings. It is the only sure way."

"Prayer does nothing for me. I say everything and hear nothing."

"You must listen to what is spoken in your heart, not your ears."

"If I listened to my heart sir, you would not be so pleased."

"And why is that?" He turns to look at me now as we walk. I have his attention.

"'Tis quite dark in there, and in the worst of ways I fear."

He stands up tall, looming over me and blocking out the sun with his large frame. He smiles, places his powerful hand on my shoulder, and begins leading me back toward the center of town. "You shall receive some counseling tonight at the courtesy of Elder Vines."

"Sir, I —"

"I know you do not want to attend such a thing, but I believe it will help you greatly in your becoming quest from girl to woman," he says, removing his coat from my shoulders. "I ask of you just one meeting. That is all. He has much experience with assisting our Puritan youth and I think you shall be quite satisfied. Agreed?"

"Yes, sir."

"Good. You shall arrive at his house at nine o'clock."

"Thank you minister."

"Now go home. Prepare what you would like to discuss, write any questions you may have, and we shall do what is necessary to help you feel faithfully whole again."

"Yes, sir. Thanks be unto you."

"And to you as well, my dear."

I move quickly down the road so as to keep my blood pumping fast enough to ward off the cold. As I do, I see the minister walk back toward the meetinghouse. At the back door I see the young man from before – the one who tipped his hat, waiting. The minister approaches him, and then in an uncharacteristic fashion, he puts his arm around the young man and leads him inside.

A gust of wind sweeps by and the minister drops his hat while entering through the doorway. As he turns to stoop and reclaim it from the ground, I can see a large smile has come across his face.

CHAPTER FIVE

The meeting was brief and –" Purity's finger goes to my lips. "Shhhh. We'll talk later. For now, we run." her eyes widen with beautiful insanity at the last word and she starts off across the field and toward the forest.

A giggle escapes me. So foreign and odd it sounds that I hardly hear my own soul within the grinning squeals. I cover my mouth, embarrassed from condition of proper conduct – one which never allows such loose laughter from a girl.

"Free yourself!" Purity says as she smiles back at me. "No one is watching you!" She bounds on up ahead, deeper into the woods.

I follow with a smile stuck on my face, for she reminds me what true joy is. She appears as the love of life personified, prancing through the breaking rays of sunshine which penetrate the forest and gleam over her.

"Wait for me!" I yell to her.

"I wait for no one!" she replies without turning around.

I move faster, enjoying the rush of blood pounding from both excitement and exertion, for I haven't been allowed any play since my last sister left the house. Since then I have only lived loneliness in my orphanage prison.

She stops up ahead and in a moment I am beside her, breathless and sweaty now. I'm suddenly concerned of my appearance, for I want her to think of me as beautiful as I do her. I fix my hair best I can, wiping the damp strands away from my face.

Purity looks far below and I follow her gaze down to a most wondrous sight. Beneath us, the creek cascades over the bluff onto large, dark rocks, sending fine, sparkly mist into the air. Quite a magical scene 'tis in an otherwise bleak forest.

She turns to me and her smiling eyes say: *amazing, isn't it?*

I imagine commanding the rushing water to explode over the edge just below my feet. Standing above it makes me feel powerful.

"Sit with me," she says, kicking off her shoes.

"That water is freezing, I'm sure of it," I reply.

She looks at me daringly. "Perhaps, but 'twill make you feel quite alive. I promise."

I let out a sigh of defeat and I clumsily try to remove my shoes.

"Here, hold my hand," she says, extending it to me.

I take it and the warmth and softness sends a rushing wave through my body, as if something dead within me has been revived by her touch. I'm sure I've never felt this way before.

Purity has already descended her feet into the water and she looks at me with persuading eyes. I feel the icy prickles jumping at my skin and against my own hesitation, I plunge my feet into the water. The cold sends an immediate shiver through my body.

After a painful moment, my feet are numb and I am relaxed once again.

"I come here sometimes to get away from my life," she says quietly. "Sometimes I think of running away out here to live a natural life on my own."

"I hardly believe you'd survive," I reply, smirking. "The witches would surely find you and cook your insides for stew."

We both laugh, remembering the minister's speech from earlier.

"Sometimes I don't care to survive," she says. "I'd rather live in my own truth than a fake life of appearances. Don't pretend you never feel the same way."

"Yes, but short of living amongst the natives, how would you ever do it?"

"I'm not saying I ever will, Verity. I'm simply dreaming, wishing upon what could be I suppose."

"Why do you choose this spot?" I ask.

She looks at me and smiles coyly. "You would think it to be a stupid reason."

"Oh? I am far stranger than you shall ever know," I say, laughing once again.

"I believe that when the woods wash my feet, they wash my sins away as well," she says in a more somber tone. "As Jesus did with the disciples the night before his death."

"You believe in such a ritual?"

"I believe in the significance," she replies. "There's something magical in feeling reborn out here. It's important to be touched by nature."

"To be quite honest, I don't believe in anything we read at church."

"Nor do I very often," she says. "My ideas go far beyond what could be contained in a single book. I believe in a spirit much greater than those words could ever convey. After all, they wrote no part for one like me to live a life according to the scripture anyway."

"What do you mean?"

"The trees never judge us," she says, staring off into the unending oak-columned landscape.

"Can you understand why sometimes I think of running away?"

"Yes, but what of your husband?"

"He doesn't love me. He barely notices when I am gone. He has his own life that he tends to."

"Does that not bother you?"

"Not one bit – I enjoy my lovely freedom," she replies. "Besides I cannot judge his life, for he is quite like myself and has his secrets as well."

I slide in closer to her. "What secrets?"

"'Tisn't appropriate for me to share." She appears a bit disgusted. "Just know that our marriage is more one of protective appearances, not just for myself, but for him as well."

Deciding not to push her any more, I instead take in the moments spent with her lavishly, appreciating every passing breath as if it were more valuable than gold. Beside me sits a lovely friend, one who brings smiles out of my heart and races my pulse with nervous excitement and I feel as if patience shall be the only way to earn her trust. Such things take time and time alone.

I feel different with Purity. There is a quality to her that begs something of my soul.

Sickness envelopes me for but a moment, likely remaining from years of proper conditioning to be "holy." I quickly push it aside, for it feels right to be with her. I've never admired a girl this way before. I think this may be all in my head but I feel so strongly for her. Perhaps 'tis because we are so very different from everyone else.

She looks to me with loud, loving eyes – as if she reads my mind. She takes my hand. "Life is hard, Verity. Now that we've found one another, we must stay together, for there are hardly any others in this colony who would understand us."

"'Tis why I opened up myself to you in service earlier," I reply. "Because I knew in my heart you felt the same way about this life as I. I feared it might have been my only chance to make a true friend."

"And now we have each other," she says, taking my other hand while the waterfall crashes on.

**

"Fancy, isn't it?"

My eyes drop into the cup of tea that Purity's just placed in my hands. Circular ripples of hot, murky water move outward and disappear against the cup's wall. Tiny seeds that resemble dead mites float to the top and I decide this drink looks very unpleasant.

"There's blackberries in it," she says with a justifying smile. "Blackberries and other things. I made it myself, so don't be too harsh."

My eyes come back up and she's moving toward me from

across the kitchen. She kneels in front of me and places her hands on my knees, looking up at me in such a way that a servant might in front of a master. My hand trembles more.

"Please try it for me?" she says through a convincing pout. "I promise 'tis poison free and very good for you. Actually, I do believe I've never shared this drink with anyone before." She stands in front of me, re-assuming her power position and smiling once again. "This is quite a privilege, young lady. You should be honored to try it. Go on then."

The drink goes down smoothly – cinnamon, berries, and warm honey all converge into a rather wonderful mix that would hardly come to be expected by any person who looked into the off-putting cup.

"So what did he say?" She lowers herself expectantly into the chair across from me.

"Well… 'twas about a few *concerns* he had for my faith."

"Oh really? What happened? Was he mad?" The questions come one after another.

"No," I reply. "He wasn't mad. Rather, he seemed especially concerned about me. Why would a minister waste such time on someone far less involved in the goings-on of the colony? I'm just a girl."

"Hmmmm," she narrows her eyes at me. "Perhaps he feels like you are more than that. Perhaps he gives such attention to those who need it. Maybe he believes you have something more to offer?"

"I don't believe that. Must've been Goodmother who appealed to him since I'm the only one at the orphanage for her to bother with anymore."

"Perhaps the *last* one," she says.

"What?" I ask. "The last one?"

"I hear rumors. Josiah spoke of the minister proposing to end funding of the orphanage."

"But why?" I ask, surprisingly saddened.

She looks down. In Salem, downward eyes look like sadness, but feel like fear. "The minister spoke of how unclaimed babies bring bad things," she says hesitantly. "He says a baby left without a mother is but a vessel for Satan, and therefore…" She sighs to clear the air. "Musn't stay."

Fury fills my blood. "How could he? That just isn't true, Purity! Satan isn't real!"

Purity's eyes stay where they are. "You don't know that, Verity. The minister is just doing what he thinks is right."

"Oh do not *side* with that man against me," I reply. "You know it – you know that 'tis all lies. You cannot hide your doubts from me. I've already felt them from you."

"You are still young," she says. "I know you're smart. I know your mind expands very far, but you do not know it all. None of us do. We must trust the minister sometimes, for the decisions he makes may benefit the greater people."

"You believe killing babies is quite fine then?"

"I did not say that, Verity."

"Lest you forget I'm one of those babies," I say. "I thought you were my friend."

"I did not say I agree with his decision," she responds softly. "I only mean we must support the decisions of those we trust to lead us."

"No, we must stop terrible things like this," I reply. "Sitting with our heads down makes us guilty."

"You cannot win a war against the Minister, Verity, not if the people side with the decisions of the church. And how dare you say I'm not your friend. I'm allowed to differ in beliefs, and I do not believe that killing babies is alright."

"Do you believe Satan is real?" I ask.

"No," she says, "but I believe in darkness."

The front door rushing open interrupts my reply. A man I presume to be her husband shuts the door behind him and raises his eyes to us. I recognize him immediately.

He's the one who the Minister led into the meetinghouse after our walk. A fair boy with a forlorn way about him, I wonder how he can always look so somber whilst being married to Purity.

His surprise to see me sitting in his home is obvious, but there's something else in his eyes too. He looks... afraid.

"Hello, husband," Purity says with a smile that dashes away the ominousness of our conversation. "How was your meeting?"

With his coat huddled against his skeletal neck and his eyes large and glassy brown, he looks quite like a mouse, twitchy and fearful of everything around him. "Fine," is all he replies.

Purity rolls her eyes and smiles at me. "This is Verity, my new friend. She's staying for some tea. Would you join us please?"

Hardly acknowledging her, he removes his coat, places it on a hook on the wall, then comes and takes a chair beside his wife.

She does not look toward him. "Verity, my husband Josiah." She gestures exaggeratedly toward us both.

They seem so far away from one another.

"How do you do, sir?" I reply.

He nods.

"Verity lives over in the Bridge Orphange," she says. "We acquainted with one another during service today and had a rather wonderful time enduring the exceptionally bleak sermon that Minister Barrowe shared this morning. Wasn't it dreadful?" She looks at me for approval.

"Aye," I reply, relegating myself to a standard response while I want to say so much more.

"I'm glad you made it home before nightfall, husband," she says, still looking at me. "No telling when that demon out there will try to make one of us the next topic of sermon."

We all look to the front door for a wondering moment.

"So," Purity looks at me with a half-smile, "Verity over here is quite interested in all things pertaining to religion, magic, and the like. I told her how studious you are. Can you share of your lessons tonight?"

Josiah settles into his chair and sighs, piecing together thoughts as he contemplates what next to say. His mannerisms declare that he hasn't a choice. 'Tis odd, for he is the man yet seems to follow what she says. "Well, tonight we spoke of how to minimize hysteria and what to do about this evilness parading through our village which has claimed our livestock."

"Oh?" Purity makes a face that she is comically enticed. "Is it a witch, a demon, or the devil himself?"

"I do not mind either way," I reply. "I think 'tis exciting to wonder."

"It isn't exiting," Josiah says quietly. "It's only dangerous and we musn't allow things like this to infect the colony. The minister believes that we open ourselves too much to unpleasant thoughts and attract these things to us. Be vigilant in your thoughts."

"I think a witch is responsible," Purity declares with folded arms, sitting upright like an official of congress.

Josiah looks at her.

"A *secret* witch."

I let out a quick laugh, but hush it when I see how unamused Josiah is.

"He's always getting stern with me because he thinks my interest in witches is unhealthy, or *strange* perhaps?" She side-eyes him and smirks. "I think the history is remarkably interesting and I believe in them." She turns to challenge him with her statement. "I even believe at least one is here in Salem, Josiah. What do you have to say about that?"

"I think we shouldn't worry," he says. "It's for the church to handle, but I do not think there are witches among us."

She smiles at me. "I have a book on their history if you'd like to borrow it. I must've read it a hundred times now."

"Absolutely, thank you," I reply.

"Wait here," she says.

Purity leaves the room with haste and immediately the air grows cold and awkward as Josiah and I are left in silence with one another. Being presumably too much for him to handle, he gets up and walks into another room without a word.

She returns with a large book, emerald green and faded but adorned with brilliant silver accents trimming the covers. "This here is all the history I could ever find on witches. You'll love it." She sets it in my lap.

"I appreciate this very much," I reply. Then a sad thought comes over me. Other than a bible, I have never in my life read *any* other book.

"Read it quickly so we can talk about it," she says with a gleaming smile.

"I will." I stand up, hoisting the heavy book into my small, cradling arms. "I must be going now. I have to prepare for my meeting tonight."

"I'm sorry for what Josiah said."

"No need," I reply. "He's only telling his truths. All things end, right?"

"Sadly, yes."

"Goodnight, Purity. I'll see you soon."

Closing the door behind me, I venture out into the dusky evening chill of the quickly darkening village. Though some sunlight still slivers its way over the horizon, the streets are mostly empty. Since the elder spoke of the unknown evil in our woods, the residents of Salem have been turning in much earlier, well before the sun sets. One man goes by, quickly leading a horse and looks at me for a long moment, either wondering why I'm outside, or wondering if I'm the monster.

I smile at him, but in my mind, I pretend that I am.

CHAPTER SIX

I place the book up in a dusty, hidden corner of my room, tucked behind the ceiling rafter where my sisters and I would hide rocks that we thought could be arrowheads from the spear tips of natives that used to inhabit the land this house sits upon. I move to the door, claim my cloak, and swing it around my shoulders, the dense wool warming my skin to a sweat almost immediately. I head down the stairs, through the scripture room and into the kitchen, where Goodmother is pouring some ale from a pitcher.

"I shall be heading to the meetinghouse now."

She looks to be quite content in witness of my obvious misery.

"The minister's faith is admirable. Most would not send a child out into the night amidst such frequent horrors."

"I suppose his faith is one we should all admire." I snap.

Goodmother smiles at me. She knows well of my detest toward such things.

I make my way toward a table on the far side of the kitchen, one in which assorted potatoes are all lain out for washing, freshly dug and speckled with dirt. I grab a clean basket usually used for collecting vegetables.

"I think well of seeing a man trust in the lord the way he does," she says, barely before finishing a swig of drink. "Perhaps when God leads you through the night and safely home, you shall think more of him too."

I place the bible in the basket, eyeing the knife that Goodmother has designated for animal skinning sitting at the edge of the table. I should take it, for I believe God will not drop one from the sky should I need it for protection against the unseen monster of Salem.

"And if I should end up scattered about the village in bloody pieces?"

"Well, I shall merely collect what remains and bury you as such," she says, laughing to herself. "What else am I to do?"

"Nothing I suppose." I see her turn to grab the pitcher once again. I quickly slide the knife off of the table and into the basket, grabbing the bible and replacing it on top in order to hide it. "I only ask of you not to say any prayers for me, for if I am dead, I need no such things anymore and I surely don't want them haunting whatever is left of me." I head toward the door. "I will leave you to your ale now."

Before she can reply, I throw open the door and step outside, closing it promptly behind me and closing off whatever retort she had.

The vast stillness of the night is nothing if not ominous.

***

My angst disappears into the foggy dark, but 'tis swiftly replaced by fear. The lingering moisture in the air has become a ghostly grey sheen, abstracting all of the familiar forms around me into things more demonic. 'Tis as if another world appears when the sun sets. I watch as parked wagons shift into carriages of the underworld. Peaceful-eyed horses, chestnut brown in the daylight, morph into black shadow stallions, snorting their hot breath into the air, restless to race their evil riders across the village to claim any God-fearing villagers who stray.

The road seems longer than ever before. 'Tis not but a half mile or so – a rather short walk and regularly traveled by myself, but in the soft glow of the harvest moon, the road looks to be leading not toward the other side of the village, but toward a dark nothing.

Should I be traveling this alone?

Wasting no more time, I begin to walk briskly, pulling my cloak around my shoulders and my bonnet down over my eyes. I wore all dark colors tonight and can only hope it helps me to not be seen by any lurkers.

I pass by rows of houses to my right, some familiar, others not. Each one shelters different people living the same mundane life, never feeling the real tragedy of their complacency. This is the curse of the people of Salem Village and perhaps everywhere else.

A door opens from a house up ahead and a young girl steps outside to dump a pot of water onto the grass. She must hear my footsteps crunching against the road pebbles, because she rises straight up from her bent over position, peering toward my direction as if she's a fearful doe listening for a wolf. I say nothing to her, but she must realize me to be only a young girl and not some wandering demon, because I can see her relax as she continues her chore, which is now scrubbing the contents of the held pot.

Keeping in stride, I pass Grace's house, my former sister. For how close we live to each other, I rarely see her anymore. She has had a child since, and her husband John is hardly the conversing type. I suppose it is meant to be that ones we love pass through our lives, remaining with us only when there is some reason for them to be there, and then they fade away and their promises leave with them.

As each minute passes and I remain safely on my way, I start to feel much less afraid of the woods. Anticipating a stare from the blazing eyes of some unknown demon stalking me from within the darkness, I grow quite annoyed at my imagination for conjuring up such horrors when all I've seen on this walk so far is nothing –

Until now.

My heart turns and my bones freeze still.

There's a moving shadow.

Walking toward me through the fog.

Who would be out here tonight?

Stop being dramatic, I tell myself. *'Tis just another villager out here like yourself.*

I tremble a bit, but I don't miss a step. I will just keep my head down, keep moving forward. It's just us out here, but if I scream, someone will surely hear. I slip my hand into the basket, under the bible and onto the knife I brought with me.

He's closer to me now. I should hear his footsteps on the gravel but I don't. Maybe he *is* a ghost. Or Lucifer himself.

He's tall – considerably so. He could overwhelm me in a blink.

Gripping the knife, I prepare myself. I start to say a prayer, but I stop myself. What would I say anyway?

He's close now; ten steps away. Not sure of my abilities with a knife, I take a moment to try and envision how I should use it.

Seven steps – six – five –

Stab it into his neck, I tell myself. As if the devil would be stopped by such a thing.

He's right in front of me now, but I still can't see him. Head down, hood up, long shadows of dark hair about his face, I can see none of his features. His clothes are peculiar though. Not of typical Puritan wear, he looks... like a soldier. His boots seem of combat style, clinking buckled spurs upon the road, with a metal plate across the front where they bend. Old European perhaps. A long cloak covers the rest of his body, making him little more than a shadow.

He's upon me now. I'm ready...

I hold my breath, then I look up and our eyes meet for just a moment. His gaze peers through his dark hair and into my soul.

Then he passes me by. His aura, colder than the nighttime air, chills me as he moves beyond without speaking a word. I keep myself moving on course, resisting every urge to turn around and steal one more glance. Finally succumbing to this desire, I turn.

He's gone.

Stopped now in the road, I look everywhere.

How strange. What I could see of his face looked young, but older than I. His presence, while certainly cold, felt absent of evil. Surely, this man could not be the devil, for he did nothing to hurt me. Intrigued as I am to figure out the mystery of the dark ghost man, it is important I keep on toward the church, for I cannot be late if I am to make an appropriate impression.

I turn back onto the path, still trembling and very alert. I can see the large meetinghouse in the distance. Just behind it are little squares of yellow light glowing from the elder's house, indicating that he must be there and waiting. I almost jog now, trying to hurry the last stretch of the walk. As the road broadens and the woods to my left recede into the bending night, I spot a single light of incandescence in the shallow part of the forest. It's likely now, that whatever is haunting us, surely lives in the woods, and the only known resident of them is a man who is as much legend as he is flesh. A man named Silas Mather.

Old man Mather's house – or "the Devil's house," as the young children say, has been the subject of many scary stories told to one another in bed at night. For reasons unknown, he was all but banished many years ago. Rarely seen outside, he never speaks to anyone and no one goes to visit with him. Reduced to living out his days in a little shack set far into the woods, he will most likely die there, only to be found years later when someone stops by to negotiate purchase of his land or something of the sort. I've never seen him before and I wonder what he knows of the dweller in the woods.

I thought I would feel more relieved to arrive safely, but my thoughts linger with the stranger. Hopefully, this counseling session will be brief and then perhaps I may be able to explore the night a bit more before going back to the orphanage.

I reach my hand out to open the door when off in the distance, I hear a most horrific sound.

A horse.

Panicked bleating turns to screams, then stills to silence.

CHAPTER SEVEN

Hurry in, child. 'Tis cold as death out there tonight," Elder Vines says as he steps back in an overly polite manner, motioning for me to enter in the way a servant might for a princess.

I step cautiously into his home with profiling eyes, taking in the details around. I'm amazed and appalled by the conditions of the elder's living. No wife, no children, yet the space to house a family of ten, and neatly stacked firewood as well. I believe his home to be even bigger than the orphanage itself, and I am quite surprised that he needn't any negroes at this time to maintain its keeping.

The demand for slaves within the colonies has been rising as of late and how terribly cruel I see such a thing. Can one righteously speak of God's mercy then shackle his father's people? I do not know of this man's opinion on such a matter, but he seems to be the type that speaks of them as nothing more than laborious animals to his peers while they laugh and clank ale mugs together in humor. I sense this is in his nature and I see it in his eyes.

"Tea?" he says, closing the door behind me in a delicate way.

"Oh," I reply, surprised when his hands come up around my shoulders to my neck, undoing the lace of my cloak. "'Tis very kind of you sir, but no thank you."

He reaches his slender fingers down to the front, too near of my breasts, then sweeps the covering wool open and swings it off my shoulders in a swirling dash. He hangs it up on a hook near the front door then stares at me for a moment in a strange way. He smiles and I feel absolutely naked.

"Forgive me that I could not see you earlier," he says, motioning to neatly stacked piles of papers which cover the surface of an expensively polished writing desk. "The ministry keeps me quite busy in these most hectic of times."

"Quite alright, sir."

"Worry not though, I shall keep this brief for us," he says, stepping over to the kitchen where he pours himself some tea. "Fore it becomes too late and too frightening for you to leave."

"'Tis only frightening if you are of a four legged nature, sir," I reply.

"Indeed. I 'spose you do have a point." He stirs something into his cup then makes his way over to where I have remained standing in proper respect. "Without wasting any more time then, to the study room?" He holds out his free hand in request of mine.

I lay my hand in his, surprised when I feel it to be warm. His long, slender fingers have a pale, dead look to them, as if they would only ever be cold. How inordinate 'tis to hold hands this way. Something feels strange here. I suddenly realize I'm breathing quickly now, pulse rising by the second. I feel sick.

I cannot banish Hope's death from my mind.

He leads me to the stairs in a gentlemanly manner and I expect him to walk up ahead of me, but he doesn't. Instead, he stops and places his hand on the small of my back and gently pushes me onto the first step.

"Go on up, child."

The rising stairwell is dark and imposing. "I hardly know where to go, sir."

"I'll tell you, go on."

Staring up the stairs as if they lead to a morbid abyss from where I will never return, my instincts scream to run back down the stairs, knock him from my path, and bolt out into the darkness. But I can do no such thing to a ministry official. I have no choice but to obey, afraid though I am.

I draw in a large breath then take a step. I climb another. Then one more.

"A little slower, my dear," he says, a stern chill now to his voice.

Looking up in dread, I feel as if I'm ascending the steps of the village execution platform, as if I'm to be hung when I arrive at the top. I haven't any reason to believe harm is about to come to me, but I do. He did not sentence her death, but only facilitated the carrying-out of it. And yet I cannot escape the feeling that he is gravely dangerous. These thoughts are probably nothing more than uncomfortable irrationality, but I shan't ignore my own heeding.

I take a couple more steps, and finally I arrive at the top. I look left, then right. There's a soft glow on the wall to my left, indicating some light flickering from a room to that side. Everything else is dark.

"To your left now, the room with the candle," he says from below.

I feel his eyes on me still, and even though I'm fearful to walk toward the study room, any escape from his gaze burning on my back is a welcome risk.

I walk down the short hallway and I can now hear his boots thudding on the stairs, each step creaking as he pulls his weight off and onto the next with another thud. I hurry to the end of the hall, and I quickly enter the room.

I want to take advantage of every moment I have to think. Something is very wrong. *Search the room*, I tell myself. *Find something, anything that you may use as a weapon.* Hopelessly, I scavenge about. I see only books lain around, a small bench…

The knife! It's in my basket still – downstairs. How careless of me.

He's reached the top of the stairs.

Without any time left to fight the situation, I decide it best to relax myself; to breathe as softly I can in an attempt to not look as worried as I feel. Besides, I am quite incoherent of people sometimes. I could be unrightfully afraid of this man.

I place myself on the bench, trying to appear calm. I fold my hands so as not to show their trembling and do my best not to look out into the hall as if The Reaper himself is coming for my soul.

His boots thud toward the room a couple more times,

then he stops, framed in the doorway, and looks in at me. "Oh my does the candlelight bring the woman to your face, child." He smiles and takes a step into the room. He looks much bigger now. "However could I forget such beautiful occurrences?"

Still seated and frozen on the bench, I realize my back is to the wall and I'm as far into the corner of the room as possible, but it doesn't feel far enough.

He walks toward his right, into the shadows, and emerges with a large wooden chair from the corner of the room near the door. He drags it toward me, grinding the heavy wooden legs against the hardwood floor, breaking the quiet with a loud echoing rumble. He places it close to me and sits down, creaking every fiber of the old wood.

Our eyes lock. I feel as if my life is being drained from me, but I don't look away.

"What are your fears?" he asks abruptly, the pitted crevices of his ghastly face hollowed even more by the candle's glow.

"Savages perhaps?" I answer, content to lie.

"Rightfully so," he says, smiling just from one corner of his lips. "But what of God then? Do you not fear him at all?"

"Not much, sir."

"And why not?"

"Well, he hasn't yet shown me anything to fear I suppose."

"How foolish of you to say, for the Bible is full of texts of his wrath," he says, inching his chair a bit closer to me. "Do you not read the scripture?"

"I do, sir – every day."

"Tell me then what he must do to gain your faith, rain blood upon your head?"

"That shan't be necessary, sir."

"You have me believing differently."

I look down into my lap, avoiding his unnerving gaze. "I have fears, sir. I just don't keep foolish ones"

"And you also believe it to be foolish to fear this demon of our nights? That is what you said but a moment ago, that only animals need be afraid of Satan?"

"They've been the only ones harmed, have they not?"

"But do you know for certain whether this demon plans to kill one of us soon?"

"No sir, I don't."

He leans in closer to me and I try not to pull away. "Such an unpredictable thing is the devil. Never be so brazen to believe you know his motives." His face falls grim. "For he may just choose to kill you tonight."

My blood ices over. Something in the way he speaks unsettles my insides.

"Do you understand?"

"Yes, sir."

"Wonderful," he says, relaxing back into his chair as if he's eaten a satisfying meal. "Now in assessment, I believe your issue of faithlessness falls upon your hesitation to bare yourself appropriately."

"I – I'm not sure I understand, sir."

"To show yourself in truth, child. 'Tis how we have a relationship with God."

"As in prayer?"

"Not quite," he says, shifting forward eagerly, elbows on knees once again. "Shall we try an exercise?" He can barely contain his grin.

"Is such necessary, sir?" I say, trying not to sound pleading. "If you shall just tell me what it is I need to do, I promise you I shall do it."

"Why, that's precisely what I'm speaking of," he says, sitting up straight. "Stand now."

I do as I'm told. So tall is he that we are almost eye to eye with each other even though he has remained seated.

"Walk over toward the candle a bit closer so that I may see you better."

I do as he asks, now in great fear of what will come out of his mouth next, for I sense the impending pattern.

"I know 'tis of great difficulty to be open and honest with yourself, and with God," he says. "Such a thing is hard even for the most devout of Puritan followers and especially hard for children."

My trembling, since ceased, begins again.

"Shame is the burden carried by sinners, and we are all born sinners," he says. "Ridding ourselves of such shame remains a sure path to salvation. Free from our sins, we can then witness the true glory of God without the Devil's cloth before our eyes."

I search my racing mind desperately for something to say, a way to avoid this. I can find nothing but abstract thoughts and soundless words, broken by the horrific fear welling up from my soul and into my strained throat.

"So then, for the sake of your redemption, I shall represent God since I am a man of holy position." He extends his hand out toward the candle beside me. "This flame over here shall be my light; my Godly divinity, which shall wash over you, cleansing you of your sins."

"Sir, if you may grant me some time to reflect, I would rather speak to the minister himself another day, for it is getting quite late," I say, thankful that words have found my tongue once again.

"I would, however the minister is quite busy with the boys. Thus, he has granted me the duty of working with the girls of the village."

There is no way out.

"Now, before it grows even later, let us commence and wash your sins," he says, crossing his legs and his arms. "Remove your bonnet first. Then your blouse."

I slowly slide my bonnet off of my hair, stealing every stalling second I can, and I drop it to the floor. I feel so naked already.

"Shake your hair out, child. Free it from restraint."

I do so, back and forth as my long black hair flies side to side, fracturing my view of the candlelit room with each sharp pass it makes in front of my view. I let it come to a fall in front of my face, a wall between me and this evil man.

"Move your hair back now. Let me see your delicate face within its frame."

I do as he tells me, for what choice do I have? As I push it away from eyes, I glare at him with every bit of hatred within me. I try my best to kill him with it, concentrating every pulse of energy I have to stop the unrighteous beating of his heart.

He coughs a couple times. "Your topcoat now. Undo it."

He leans forward, his face seems to show pain, wincing strangely as if he's being jabbed by a blade.

Starting at the top, I unbutton each of the four buttons one at a time, down the row of separation between my breasts. I am numb now. Numb to every feeling except the deep burning embers of hate blazing deep inside of me.

"Open it! Show yourself to me!" He yells, rasp appearing in his voice. He is sweating now, his eyes wide, darting around the room with anxiety and fear.

I close my eyes. Clasping my clenched fingers around the parted folds of fabric, I prepare myself for everything – to be the object of this horrible man's show. Hate seething from my heart, pouring into every part of the room, my mind screams for this all to end.

I tear open my blouse before I can stop myself, baring my breasts as a forced offering to his evil eyes.

Opening my own eyes now, I stare at him defiantly, if only to show I'm not afraid.

But he's no longer in the chair – it sits empty.

Confused, I hurriedly close my blouse, looking to the floor. He lies face down in a heap on the cold hardwood to the right of the chair, arms folded underneath him, clutching his chest. I rush over and stoop down beside him.

No pulse. He's most certainly dead – but how?

I couldn't have possibly killed him.

***

I bolt out into the freezing air in a confused panic. What kind of nightmare has this evening become? Everything around me seems rushed to an unnaturally fast pace. My feet pound hard against the ground, my mind still in flight from the dark encounter which almost came to pass. Now Elder Vines is dead and I know not why. I am petrified and confused as to – I don't even know what to do – where to go, just running. Running to anywhere.

Slow down, Verity, I say to myself. *Slow down and think. Just find help from someone, anyone.*

The physician's house!

Doctor Coverdale lives just across the street from the meetinghouse which is not but a moment's run from here. Turning around just as fast as the thought hits me, I sprint toward his home and even from the distant road, I can see light glowing inside.

The sweat clinging to my skin feels icy now. I am barely protected by a half undone blouse and without my cloak. I must appear to be a crazy girl, disheveled and only partially dressed, running about the town in such a petrified state.

I can only hope the doctor believes what I'm about to tell him.

Arriving at the front door of his home, I slam my fist upon the cold-stiffened mahogany. "Help! Please Doctor Coverdale!" I continue pounding my fist on the door, which makes far less noise than I had thought, the dense wood absorbing most of the force while producing little sound. "Help! 'Tis urgent, sir!"

Suddenly, the door opens and Goody Coverdale is standing before me in her evening dress. The concern in her eyes tells me I went to the right place. "Good lord, child. What is the matter?" She places her hand behind my back which quickly becomes a motherly embrace as she guides me into the home. "Please come in and tell me."

I resist the urge to collapse into her arms. "No. I need the doctor. There's been an incident," I say through panting breaths as I support my hands on my knees, bracing myself while I attempt to recover my wind. "It's Elder Vines – I... I believe he's dead."

"Oh heavens. Wait here, I'll fetch him immediately," she says before rushing up the stairs in a dash.

For the first time since I ran from the house, the entirety of the nightmare which has just taken place begins to settle into my mind. How awfully disgusting of him – how very horrible 'twas to ask such unholy things of me in the name of God. I am not happy that he's dead, but I am grateful that I was spared from that fearful experience. However, in the absence of reason, another thought finds its way in, one that carries with it a new fear.

What if they believe 'twas I who caused his death?

Nonsense. Doctor Coverdale will rule such a thing out, for it was probably a cause quite obvious to a medical man such as he. Given the terrified state I was in after all, I surely did not notice what had happened, for I wanted only to escape from Elder Vines and did so when his sudden death granted me the chance.

Footsteps hurrying down the stairs brings me back to appropriate presentation as I upright myself while futilely attempting to make adjustments to my appearance. Hair brushed back, blouse straightened, I do not want the doctor to see me in such a shameful state.

The doctor appears on the stairs first, followed by his wife. He steals a quick glance at me and then at the unsightly nature of myself, hurries even quicker down the remaining steps. "What has happened?" he asks as he approaches, throwing a coat around his shoulders.

"Elder Vines, sir – he's dead I believe."

"But what has happened?" he says impatiently. "How did he die?"

"We were in his house, sir, upstairs. He just fell out of his chair. I tried to aid him, but he was dead already, so I ran straight here to get help."

"And you are?" he asks.

"Verity Bridgemaiden, sir. I reside at the ministry orphanage."

His eyes flash sadness for a moment, for 'twas he who pronounced my sister dead after her hanging and I see that old pain come forward for just a moment before retreating. He runs into another room then re-enters the foyer just as quickly with a bag which I assume to be a medical satchel. "Let us hurry over there. Perhaps there's still time." Throwing open the front door, he bounds out into the night with the gait of a soldier, armed for battle once more against the adversary named Death.

I start to follow, but am stopped by Goody's hand on my shoulder.

"Wait, child. Let us get you a coat," she says, making her way to a row of hooks holding various outer garments. She pulls down a red one and hands it to me. "There you go, dear. Now we may leave."

I toss it over my bare shoulders, only now realizing the cold that was lingering in my bones. We step out into the darkness, and Goody slams the door tightly shut behind us. I see the doctor already far ahead – nearly to Elder Vines' house. We start off on the road, our feet unintentionally pacing in perfect marching unison. Dread begins to creep into my gut once more, a threatening feeling like what I had felt at the Elder's house. I feel it slide into the back of my mind – this thought that I am somehow marching toward my own execution.

"What were you doing at the elder's house, child?" Goody asks.

Taken aback by a question I should have prepared myself to answer, all words escape me at once. I know not whether to say the truth or lie in the better interest of a dead man, for he is no longer a threat and ruining the image of a man of God will bring much unwanted detest from the people. My silence draws concern onto Goody's face, so I simply stare at the ground I walk upon in silence.

"You are but a young girl and you were at the elder's house at such a late hour, and for what reason?" she asks, more persistence in her voice now.

I remain vigilant with my chosen silence, my eyes not averting from my feet.

"Why can't you look at me?" she asks. "What happened there tonight? You must tell, child. Before we arrive."

I look up, only to realize we are approaching the elder's home. There is not enough time to explain everything to her – not a story as extravagant as mine and with such an unexplainable death concluding the event. I know in my heart

I should tell her, for we are alone and she may have some influence and credibility to protect my integrity, if only by being the doctor's wife. Yet there is no time for it. "We had a bible counseling session," is all I can muster.

"Counseling? At this time of night?" she asks, clearly not believing my story. "That is a lie. Shall you tell me the truth now please?"

I let out a long sigh. "No." I continue walking with her, head up now as we approach the front door. "I shall speak of this another time."

"Fine then," she says. "We shall talk of this tomorrow and I want you to tell me everything. Understood?"

"Aye."

She opens the door, and upon entering, the smell of his house returns to me like a knife slicing through my body. It carries with it every vivid, hellacious detail of the previous events between myself and the elder. We immediately move toward the stairs, and I notice my basket still resting on the small table near the bottom of the stairwell.

Hurrying up the steps, each one reminding me of my earlier uncertainty, I feel myself becoming breathless, rising anxiety penetrating my lungs and pushing the air aside. I think I may faint. We arrive to the top and Goody stops, unsure of which side of the hallway to start down.

I politely slink in front of her. "This way," I say as I make my way down the hall toward the horrible room where I hope he still lies dead. My answer is granted as I round the doorway only to see Doctor Coverdale covering the body of Elder Vines with a white sheet. He then stands up and crosses his hands in front of himself for a moment, his eyes blinking back tears, or perhaps sleepiness, from behind the round lenses of his glasses.

He turns to me as his wife appears by my side, both of us now staring eagerly at him for an answer.

"A heart event I suppose," he says matter-of-factly. "Unusual for a man his age. Yet it remains the only rational conclusion given the circumstances, for it is either a bad heart or the devil's work."

"A heart event? But John, he's barely older than us," Goody says, not quite believing that to be the cause.

"I know. Doesn't make much sense to me, but such things happen from time to time," he replies, still looking at the sheet-covered mound on the floor. He then brings his investigative eyes to mine. "Are you sure nothing else happened, Verity?"

I glance over my shoulder to Goody and she peers back at me with disappointment before I look back to the doctor. "No, sir. Nothing else."

"Very well then," he says with resolution in his voice. "I shall take care of the body and inform Minister Barrowe of this misfortune." He kneels down beside his bag and removes a large spool of thin rope. "Sarah, you may take the girl home now and tell her caretaker what has happened."

"Yes, John," she replies.

From downstairs, the front door shudders open, bringing with it a loud boom as it slams against the wall. Heavy boots thunder against the stairs as multiple men make their way up to the room, shaking the wooden floor beneath our feet.

I turn away from the room to look down the hall in witness

of who shall appear at the top of the stairs. Suddenly, a hulking figure appears in the darkness, rising from the stairwell and into the hallway. Stepping from the shadows and toward the candlelight flickering on the walls, the figure approaches the room, followed now by two other men. The light now reveals who it is.

Minister Barrowe.

And his eyes are roaring with anger.

"What has happened here?" Barrowe says with stern command in his voice.

The warm comfort that I had felt with Goody beside me is suddenly pulled away from my soul like a cozy blanket torn from my body in the middle of a wintry night, leaving me exposed to the uncertain elements. Leaving me exposed to the minister.

He approaches us with an air of grave intentions, leaving me nowhere to run, only the brief opportunity to collect myself in attempt to hide all emotion from my face.

"Elder Vines is dead, sir. My husband thinks it to be a heart attack," Goody says as if to speak first in hopes of protecting me.

I feel my attempt to be in vain as I flush with fear.

"Step aside, Goody," he orders as he stops in front of me. He peers straight into my eyes with a stone-turning look. "You tell me now, and you tell me the truth, child. What have you done here?"

"Nothing, sir. I have done nothing," I manage to tremble out of my mouth in a voice quieter than I expect.

He bends down to my level to stare at me for a moment

more and it feels like an eternity. He doesn't blink, yet the little muscles at the corner of his jaw begin to flex as he grinds his teeth together with hidden fury. "Lies," he whispers. "You dare lie to me?"

He snatches my arm with an alarming power and I'm dragged into the main study room where Doctor Coverdale has been writing upon a paper tablet, probably things related to the death of the elder. He pulls me over to the white sheeted body which lies still upon the floor at my feet.

"What have you done to this man?" Barrowe yells. "Tell me. You tell everyone, for your responsibility in this crime must be confessed to all."

"Do not accuse me sir, for I have told the truth!"

The minister turns toward Doctor Coverdale, still holding my arm in his iron grip. "You say a heart attack, doctor?"

"Yes, sir. I do believe it was, for I see no visible signs of damages otherwise."

"That I do believe," he says, glaring back at me once more. "For Satan does not always mark his crimes. Does he, child?"

"I am innocent, sir! I have done nothing of what you think. He simply died while we were studying – ill of heart as Doctor Coverdale has determined."

"'Tis what *I* determine that matters here, for God speaks through me, and I alone shall pronounce his word and lay his judgments."

Goody pushes past the men in the hall and enters the room. "Minister sir, she is but a young girl. These dark events of the past few months have us all a bit worried – perhaps unreasonably so."

"Satan shall disguise himself as an angel of light, says second Corinthians," he exclaims in his bellowing sermon voice. "Now hear ye as I say Satan lurks everywhere. He will disguise himself in the most innocent way, and he may manifest his dark presence in any one of us!" He points his finger at me. "Even within children such as she."

It all makes sense now.

The minister knew of what was to happen tonight. He knew of Elder Vine's horrible plans to undress me and have his way. He knew the elder could use his fellowship power to do so without resistance from me. Yet he can stand here and command the room to turn against me and I know he shall not stop until he receives confession from my lips.

Confession that I have killed this man, a confession which I fear somehow may actually be true.

"The elder's intentions were unholy ones!" I pronounce. "He tried to claim my innocence, yet died before he could do so!"

The room goes silent after a quick gasp.

The minister quickly regains himself from his surprise and moves toward me menacingly. "You self-exalting malicious little creature. You attempt to blind our minds. You try to make yourself a victim? Well, we shall not listen to your venomous words, for the Lord's word is all we shall heed tonight."

"You knew of it, minister. You knew what was to happen here," I say, fearless enough to draw another gasp from the surrounding listeners.

"Speak no more, you hellish orphan. Now it is clear why you know not who your parents are. It is because you have none. You were born into Salem when Satan opened the underworld only to leave your little demon self with us."

"If I am from Hell, then I shall see you soon enough, monster," I reply.

Crack!

Slammed across the face with the back of his large, powerful hand, I fall to the wooden floor, ears ringing, dizzy and thoughtless.

"Minister!" I hear Goody scream.

"Silence Sarah!" he says. "Leave your sympathies and do not question me – 'tis time now for her judgment!"

"You cannot do that!" Goody says.

"I can and I shall. This little witch must pay for her actions."

I can taste blood in my mouth, I feel a little tear where my tooth must have ripped the inside of my lip open.

"She is not a witch. She is a child!" Goody pleads.

"Doctor Coverdale, take your wife now and leave us. The man is dead, and you may come back to collect him in a bit."

I see nothing but the minister's shined black boots in front of me. I hear the doctor's footsteps move toward the door, and he must take his wife for I hear her crying fade away from far down the hall.

My only saving defense has been removed from the minister's court. Now I fear the worst.

I start to clear my head and I roll onto my back looking right up at him, his cold eyes beating my soul with disdainful condemnation.

"Come in now, men. May you witness the witch we have been seeking."

I hear the sound of other heavy boots approaching – evil soldiers of the church who now take their place in surrounding me completely.

"This source of sin must be expelled," Barrowe says. "We shall hold sentencing for this bringer of heresy, and then we shall determine her rightful fate."

I feel all of the hateful eyes upon me, tearing my body open with their stares.

"I shall take great pleasure in your punishment," Barrowe says.

Suddenly I feel one of them spit upon me. Then one by one, they all join until they have all cast their hateful spats upon my trembling body and they finally see fit to stop, leaving me shamed and hopeless.

"Leave me now, men. Wait for me downstairs, for I shall need but a minute with this monster alone."

The men leave, and Barrowe kneels down in front of me and raises my face up so I once again can become a prisoner to his stare. "Elder Vines was to have his way with you, this you know," he says. "But what you don't know, was that he was to kill you afterward. I instructed him to dismember you and leave your bloody pieces in the street. You were to be the last orphan and the first human victim of the great devil in the woods, so we could avoid all of the *issues* we had with the last one. I'm speaking of your sister Hope of course. She was the elder's toy before you, and unfortunately for her, she became pregnant and so we had to proceed with her elimination. We, the good people of Salem, do not tolerate whores in God's land."

I hear everything he says, yet it feels unreal as his vile words pass through my numbed brain. The minister of the village finally shows a side to himself more evil than I ever imagined a man could be.

"Now I must kill you as a witch instead, if only to keep the fear among the villagers high. But before I do, I must know... how *did* you murder him?"

CHAPTER EIGHT

I have only been accused, yet they touch me as if I'm already condemned. One man on each arm, they raise me to my feet, holding me away from their bodies in disgust as if I have acquired some horrible illness they wish not to catch. What a terrible look in their eyes. Oh, how they stare at me, this little witch girl who murders churchmen.

If only it were true.

"Lead her away now, to the grounds beyond the wood line," Barrowe says.

The men begin to stir a bit in hushed groans as an air of uncertainty washes over the group. One of the men speaks.

"But what of the devil in the woods, sir?" he says. "Should we not take the girl to the meetinghouse instead where we may conduct ourselves in safety? I fear he may come for her if she is indeed of the dark realm."

The minister peers at the man for a moment, perhaps contemplating his assertion – perhaps contemplating how anyone would dare to question his word. "The villagers of Salem need not witness the events of tonight," he says. "Their misguided pity will be graced on this witch on account of her youthful disposition and such a stirring brings no benefit to us or our mission of confession."

The men go quiet and the room is returned to order again.

"He hasn't come to save the others, why would he save this one?" Barrowe says, smirking out of the corner of his mouth. "I need a man to take her away while the rest fetch the equipment." He scans the group, finally landing his eyes on one. "Josiah, come forth."

A man steps out of the small crowd of churchmen, and 'tis him, Purity's husband!

Josiah, you must help me.

"Yes, sir," Josiah replies.

Barrowe bends down and retrieves a medium sized knife from inside his boot, stands, and holds it out toward Josiah. Then he turns toward me, shooting a stern glare. "Take this with you. If the witch attempts to scream, cut her. If she runs, kill her."

Josiah takes the knife into his frail, inexperienced hands. "Yes, sir."

"I will arrive shortly with men for her confession. Wait for me there," Barrowe says.

Swung around and shoved toward the doorway, I suddenly feel less than human at the mercy of these men. Josiah appears beside me and leads me out the door, down the hall and down the stairs with a shaking grip on my arm as if he's trying to appear stronger than he really is in the presence of the other churchmen. We exit out into the cold, uncertain air of Salem, and his grip suddenly relaxes.

"Stay with me," he says in more of a question than a command, lacking any real authority.

I begin to follow him, and we walk side by side. I can see his eyes dart around, looking increasingly fearful as we move farther from the house and closer to the woods. I know he's looking for the devil that they are all so afraid of. Knowing I haven't much time to save myself, I decide it best to try my hand at gaining his assistance in supporting my case against the minister. "Josiah, you remember me, don't you, from that afternoon at your house?"

He keeps marching, just a slight wrench in his step at my statement, eyes still forward, face expressionless. "Aye."

My heart crashes into my stomach. He's going to follow the orders anyway. It matters not to him that I am his wife's friend, that we had tea just yesterday afternoon.

"Josiah, you cannot do this. We both know they're going to kill me tonight. You cannot follow these orders. Please let me go."

"Sometimes we are without choices," he says. "You killed a man; this is our law. I must abide the ministry's courts… and so must you." He tugs me along a bit faster, presumably before his conscience convinces him to free me.

"I know that you are both different." My eyes search out his, but he gives me nothing. "She has told me what your marriage hides and I know of you and the minister. You are hiding your own trespasses, are you not?"

In a small burst of anger, he whirls his head toward me. "Why do you speak of this now? Should you not be more concerned with the fate that is awaiting *you*?"

"I am concerned!" I say. "'Tis why I am pleading with you. I need your help! I need you to be in alliance with me and expose the minister for who he really is as I have done with the elder tonight. Or let me run. Please Josiah, I beg you – don't let me die tonight. There is so much yet to say and only we can say it. Change things with me. Let us bring justice together."

He looks around the village as if the families in their homes can hear our hushed words outside and far from their beds. "I'm sorry, I cannot do that. I have a quiet life. The only way I'm allowed to live in this village is to do the beckoning of the minister." He stares at the ground, a coward who'd rather send a young girl to die. His face says he's shamefully aware of what he is. "It's the only way for me to privilege myself away from sure execution."

We both stop and look in front of us, toward the edge of the blackened woods that we all remain so afraid of.

"I hope the devil takes your heart, for you don't deserve to have one."

He says nothing, just stares into the darkness.

I begin to move forward once again; his hand still gripped on my arm forces him to follow.

As we enter the perimeter of the wood line and cross into the covering dark unfolding over bare and baneful trees, a strange feeling comes over me.

The satisfaction of a dream fulfilled.

How I had always longed to enter these woods at dark. When sleep betrayed me, I would stare from my window, the midnight view capturing my imagination like a world far from attainment. Wiping my condensing breath from the glass, I would be reminded of the invisible barrier between myself and the cold unknown of the forested land where the devil dwells. If such a dark and interesting creature as he had chosen these woods to roam, then quite interesting they must be.

We continue moving. I can see the unsure fear start to overtake him as we step cautiously around thorny bushes and jagged broken sticks about our feet. The denseness of these woods seems almost calculated, as if to purposefully create much difficulty for anyone to enter. Everything is sharp and designed to cut intruders.

"Ow!" Josiah yells, likely stabbed or scraped by something in the dark.

I see the faintest of blood start to trickle down his arm, noticeable in that 'tis a bit darker than everything else. He lets go of me, freeing his hand to cover the wound. Up ahead, I notice a dim light – a house. Nestled back into the woods, I know where I am now, for it is the Mather house I can see.

Knowing I cannot rely on Josiah to help me, I decide my best option is to take a chance once more.

Before he can grab my arm again, I break away from him and fly through the trees, dodging some branches, smashing others, and running toward the light without looking back. My feet seem to move me surprisingly easily through the wooded barriers. Since there is no clear cut path, one must do their best to get through it any way they can and right now, the only thought on my mind is to make it to that house.

I can hear Josiah behind me yelling and when his voice reaches my ears, I'm surprised to hear how far off he sounds.

He must be chasing only out of duty – just enough to tell the minister he "tried" and not enough to actually catch me.

Breaking through the last bit of autumn-brittled branches, I enter a small cleared area in front of the Mather house's front steps. Not wasting any time, I run up to the front door and begin pounding on it, screaming for help.

I try the door handle – locked.

Slamming my fist against the wood, I can hear sticks cracking behind me and I know Josiah is close. I look back and see him stumble into view, clothes torn and eyes newly filled with rage.

I also see the knife, clutched tightly in his hand.

He approaches me with newfound purpose. Fear claims me and I realize that regardless of his weak spirit, he is still a soldier of the church – a man who will harm me to keep with the orders of his master.

I think of running, of beating the door some more, of crying – all of which are useless given the circumstances. Instead, I just stand my ground, showing him what it means to remain fearless against inescapable evil, showing him that he should be on my side.

A small shudder of the wood vibrates under my feet, then a low groan rocks the air as the door behind me opens. I feel the warmth of inside the home at my back and the energy of a looming figure behind me.

I turn around to face the man named Silas Mather.

***

"Step behind me now," Mather says in a voice quite less menacing than expected. He places a hand on my shoulder and moves me into the doorway, which he now blocks in confident stance on the porch, staring Josiah down all the while. Tall, but thinly built, his figure isn't the most imposing, but his status as a legend in Salem seems to be enough to keep Josiah hesitant to engage.

Josiah stops just at the front of the house, knife out and still ready. "Move aside, old man," he says in a high-pitched voice, breathless from running. "You must hand her over, by order of the church I say."

"By order of the church?" He chuckles through the long grey hair that falls about his face. "I stopped adhering to those orders a long time ago. You should as well, for there is a dark road ahead for you, boy."

Wanting to see what is to happen between these two, I peer around the man that stands between us. Josiah has stopped approaching, unsure of Silas' abilities, His knife provides nothing more than a hint of false security in the presence of this infamous man who's been demonized by years of village gossip.

"The churchmen are coming," Josiah says. "You best give her over now."

"What kind of man asks another to hand over a child in the name of duty?"

"I am but following orders myself," Josiah says. "We have no choice in this matter, but you may save yourself punishment for interfering if you just give her to me."

Horse hooves pound the ground and the rumble of weighted wagon wheels becomes present as the churchmen approach from the north, where the woods are less dense and lead toward the main road out of Salem Village.

"We always have a choice," Mather says. "You may choose to be weak son, but you shall pay for it later when you lay down to sleep, and every night after. I promise you."

Josiah turns to look in the direction of the approaching men and horses. His eyes are now ablaze with fear, for he has allowed me to escape him and instead run to the protection of this cast away man.

My care for Purity aside, I hope the minister punishes him terribly for his failure.

One by one, torches begin to light from amongst the twisting trees, illuminating the shadows of the approaching monsters. Reaching the clearing, Minister Barrowe steps forward from the darkness with a torch, leading the rest of them through the densest brush and out into the small circular patch of bare land to the right of the Mather house.

The minister walks to the center of the bare spot and sweeps his torch around it, bending to admire the ground. Then he rises back up and begins walking toward Josiah, who's still standing a few paces from us. "You remember why this spot is so bare, Silas – why nothing grows on it? why there is no life here but your wretched old self?"

"Because of your godly burnings, Lazarus," Mather replies.

"I merely burn witches." Barrowe says. "If God didn't support my cause, he would have surely stopped me from blazing all those demons away while they screamed inside his fire." He sweeps the torch down again, then holds it there for a moment, pretending to light a mound of kindling.

"Well there are no witches here tonight," Mather replies, "so you may take your men and leave now."

The wagon halts toward the edge of the bare spot, six men standing with two horses and a cart with large stones piled on top of it. Beyond the minister's torchlight which blinds me in the darkness, the men appear as black shapes – ghosts in the woods, waiting.

"I don't believe the witch is here either," Barrowe says. "However, evil has transpired tonight. Enough to warrant an interrogation of the accused." He looks past Mather, attempting to see me, yet I remain hidden quite well in the dim shadows of the home.

"What evil has happened then?" Mather asks.

"You see the horse over there – the pale one?" Barrowe asks, sweeping the torch toward the gathering behind him where a grey horse stamps impatiently in place. "That horse belonged to John Vines. Now typically we would not convene a dead man's horse, but when I went to fetch my own, I found him dead as well – drained of blood like the rest of the animals in our village as of late."

"John is dead?" Mather asks.

"Aye. Tonight," Barrowe replies. "And the accused, whom you hide, was the last to be with him." He gestures the torch toward us.

"You cannot be sure that this girl had anything to do with it," Mather says.

"No one can be sure, for only she knows the truth." The minister moves closer. "Which is why we must try for confession."

Silas Mather pushes me back a little more as the minister approaches, his cold hand now wrapping around my wrist. "If this young girl had something to say Lazarus, she would do so. This scene of yours is enough to scare any child her age into confession. Anything beyond this is simply not appropriate action by the church."

"If you were still an elder, I might consider your opinion, yet you are no longer such a man." Barrowe says, now just a few paces away. "This girl has no parents. She is an orphan – one who is cared for by *my* church." He waves behind him for other men to begin an approach as well and five or six of them begin marching toward us. "If you think I will keep funding the harboring of witches in Salem Village, you are gravely mistaken, for it is my sole duty to ensure spiritual order to our people. I care not what you think of my methods any more than I care for her tears or excuses for the crime committed."

Mather takes a step forward and I see the men around him wearing somber faces of duty. Close to the firelight of Barrowe's torch, the anticipation builds in their eyes – anticipation of knowing of their participation in hurting me.

"A good man is dead tonight and she who stands behind you was the last one with him," Barrowe says as he ascends the stairs with heavy stomps, halting face to face with Silas and towering over him with mass and height. "That murderous bitch right there killed him. That witch who stands behind you. She was borne of these woods for evil purposes, delivered by the devil's womb of eternal darkness, and you protect her."

"I protect a chil –"

Crack!

Barrowe smashes Silas in the forehead with the heavy butt of the large wooden torch he's carrying and Silas falls stiff, landing with a dead thud far louder than his thin body should make. He stands over him for a moment, admiring his work with a look of surprise at how quickly he put him down.

Silas wheezes a bit as if struggling to breathe. Then wheezing turns to low gurgling groans. He's alive, but that is all.

Satisfied with that much, but seemingly disappointed he didn't get to fight, Barrowe boots Silas' legs out of his way as if he is moving aside a few fallen pieces of furniture. His eyes seek me out in the darkness as I have backed up now into the shadows of the main room of the house. One lift of the torch however, and I am completely exposed in the glow, blazed by the crackling fire which he wields as if it had been lit by God himself.

He approaches me with diabolical mission in his steps.

"Stop, sir! I did not kill that man!" I shout helplessly.

He says nothing, grabs my arm with a grip that offers no compassion for my pain, then drags me effortlessly from the house. My dragging feet bang limply down the stairs as we hit the ground, and then in a few bounding steps, we arrive at the center of the barren spot of ground. He throws me down and I quickly roll onto my side only to see several expressionless men standing over me, eyes devoid of any humanity.

My negotiations are over.

***

I have spent my life thus far believing that there is nothing more to it but suffering. Even on a cold night when my shivering body has reclaimed its warmth from the hearth of a generous fire, my mind would still toil in painful thoughts of life and death. Love and family. Stars and heaven. Most believe that beyond the sky is a place where the righteous transcend when die. Fewer believe in something greater other than what the church preaches. The last of us believe only in the stars themselves – nothing more.

For me, the stars were always good enough.

Now I lay staring up from the ground and I can see only two images. The evil faces plastered onto the bodies of the churchmen who pin my bare limbs to the cold-hardened ground and the stars beyond their faces, glimmering from a place so far away it seems divinely surreal. A place so far, heaven may truly be the only answer for their existence.

Could they be angelic luminaries from beyond the world, lighting the way for us when we die? Should I pick out one to follow? Alas, could they be nothing more than specs of light beyond what we know, unrelated to anything biblical at all, just far-away luminescence glowing within the fathoms of the sky.

I believe…

My thoughts are broken as I am slammed by a thick slab of heavy oaken board. Breathless now, struggling for air, my head is now the only part of me left uncovered by the sheet of wood.

"Bring the stones," I hear one of them say.

Even in the cold, I feel the sweat begin to accumulate in prickly droplets on my forehead, stinging with each passing breeze. The pressure of the board labors my breathing, which now quickens in fear, for I know well of what is to come.

"She is but a young girl," I hear one man grunt with strain. "I presume the confession will come quickly enough." His final word eases out as he drops something heavy which thuds onto the dense ground to my left.

"Do not discount the resilience of evil," Barrowe replies as his boots settle inches from my head and his cold eyes peer down at me. "Lest we forget that bodily forms are nothing but disguises to trick the foolish into misguided compassion by the dweller within."

The fear in me swells to panic and my entrapment begins to feel more and more like a wooden casket with each tensioned breath I release. The weight settles on my breasts and the pain courses down through my small ribs, to my knees, then back up again. Trapped in this unforgiving situation, I feel so desperate – so hopeless.

Worst of all, no one is brave enough to stop this horror.

"Enough delay. Place the first stone," Barrowe orders.

I feel two of them approach the large stone I know is lying by my side. I hear them both grunt and then their shadows begin to crawl over me as their frames block out the minister's torchlight which had been brightening the area around my face. One of them walks around to my other side, then I feel them hesitate for a moment in contemplation of dropping a crushing stone onto a helpless young girl in the woods. Then knowing they have no choice in the matter but to carry out orders, they release it onto the board.

Hiehhhhhh is the sound that escapes me – followed by my shuddering chest straining to recapture air. My insides feel as if they are being pressed against my ribcage. The corner of the board's edge is now digging deep into my throat, making each swallow feel like a blade is inside my neck, piercing through with such force that I feel as if it may alone finish me. Tensing every muscle to relieve the weight proves useless and only causes more pressure, so I release myself and let it settle upon me with all of its force.

The torchlight approaches again, and Barrowe is standing over me. "Do you have a confession to speak, child?" He kneels down beside me, and I feel the fire on my face. "If you tell the truth in a righteous manner, you shall be absolved of this punishment and will be granted a humane trial by the courts."

I force a large breath. "I confess nothing to you."

"Stubbornness will not save you from these circumstances, for I will expel a confession from your evil lungs even if it means blessing the horses themselves so they may stand upon you," Barrowe hisses with a frustrated bite to his voice. "Speak to me, say whatever you must to save yourself from this, and we shall conduct everything in a more civilized manner."

"You know I'm not a witch."

Barrowe leans in close to my face and I feel his breath by my ear, hot enough to equal the fire. Then he lowers his voice to a whisper only I can hear. "You killed Elder John Vines. You murdered a man of my church and you *will* admit it. Whether or not you are a witch makes no difference to me. We will find you guilty of murder and you will be burned as one just the same and I will breathe of your floating ashes with much satisfaction."

He then places the torch so close to my forehead that I can see wisps of my hair become singed in the heat.

I force myself to respond, if only to show I am not weak.

"And I shall breathe of your ashes in Hell, minister."

Minister Barrowe rises and I feel the unsettling cold on my face again, my trembling stifled by the weight of the stone lain board and my eyes welling with tears at the unbearable circumstances of my inevitable death by the hands of the church. Even through struggling breath and unbearable pain, I can feel a sense of peace slowly finding its way into me.

"Another."

With barely a pause this time, a second heavy stone is placed upon me, but this time it feels much less painful, for the pressure has numbed me, as if 'tis crushing my spirit rather than my body. I start to fade into myself, the warmth laps over me like ocean waves, and I begin to part away from this event, to where it is leading me. I feel as if Death is watching, ready to come take me now.

Are the stars still good enough?

Warm liquid rises into my mouth now under the pressure of the board, still pressing mercilessly into my brittle throat. My breathing turns to wheezing and through the straining for air, I can feel blood start to run from my nose and down each cheek onto the ground.

"This wench resists all forceful pressing with a capacity granted only by means of supernatural evil!" Barrowe yells into the air with his sermon cadence. He sounds far away. "You witness now the reasons before your eyes for such heinous modes of confession. For it is God's work that we do – the banishment of evil under the same divine guidance which has brought us to this place of colonizing destiny! All men who agree say aye!"

"Aye!" the men bark in unison.

"Again – for God!" Barrowe yells.

"AYE!"

The cold seeps into the hollow crevices of my insides left untouched by the crushing board. Tunneling thoughts tumble about my mind, trampled over by the slowly descending darkness which towers over my soul, dragging me away from pain – away from life. Sleep beckons me now and I prepare for the warmth of death. My surrendering breath begins to slow.

'Tis all fading now, fading to silence…

Wait!

I cannot go yet. Not before I exclaim the truth here tonight. I must speak it now!

Suddenly I feel a scream welling inside of me, a final speech that I am to spew from my lungs in my last living breath. "Curse you all!" I cry out with all that's left in me. "I wish the fires of Hell upon your souls should they exist! You crush an innocent girl to death and you think it to be just – to be the work of God? God is dead to me! I wish for the devil you speak of! I beg that he emerges from these woods in which he haunts! If he shall be here, I ask that he come save me from this unrighteous death so I may have another chance at life – a chance for revenge against the evil of you all!"

My breath gives out and I try to take in air, but it is useless. My final moment of strength has left me empty and now I seek salvation in the sky. Death is here now, invited by my will which has fallen away.

A large shadow passes over me, blocking out the sky. I hear the screams of men. They are running and I can hear the panicked neighing of the horses, the pounding hooves as they ride away in a frenzy.

The crushing board is quickly lifted, as am I. Right into Death's embrace.

Even with the weight gone, my breath is barely present. The blood still drips from my nose and mouth, my body so weak that movement is useless. I watch the scene unfold from somewhere else. I see each jagged limb and shadowed pine pass my eyes as we move deeper into the forest. Is this the way to afterlife? My sight begins to fade even more, sleep impossible to fight any longer. This life feels too heavy. I want no part anymore.

As I die, the last image I see is a whitened speckling of a night sky which bleeds into my eternal darkness. The first snow of the season. The last of my life.

CHAPTER NINE

W hat has happened to me?" I whisper into the dark. Only no whispers come. 'Tis only a thought of mine that speaks, my lips remaining silent as the wintry powder which falls upon them. Like sticky flecks of cotton, the snow is hardly cold at all.

I attempt to find myself, to harmonize my body with my spirit, for I feel as if my bare back lies upon the snowy brush of the forest floor, but my soul hovers just above, blocked from a rightful and final descent back into my body. Two parts of me, existing separately, claw at each other as they fight for a way to unify again. I feel so lost, simply watching from a place I know not where. Trapped in-between and knowing I needn't breathe, but desiring only to do so.

"You have awakened from the poetry of your own death," a man speaks from the darkness.

Who is this stranger? How did he hear my question?

"Quite beautiful, isn't it?" he says. "Very peaceful. Not at all like death is proposed to be."

I can feel him bend down over me now, the tips of his long

hanging locks of hair tickle my face. He smells of pine. The strong scent and grazing ends do well to remind me that while I may feel a bit of a ghost this moment, I surely must be alive after all.

"You feel as if you are a girl ripped in two," he says calmly. "You try to speak – to scream, yet remain breathless all the while. So far away from yourself." He touches my face softly, running his palm down my cheek. "Believe me when I say I haven't forgotten that feeling."

Please save me from this feeling. Make me whole again.

He slips his large arms delicately under my body – one at the base of my neck, the other at the crease of my buttocks – then stands, lifting me effortlessly. Standing in the dark forest, he holds me so tightly. My tiny body engulfed completely in his embrace, he maneuvers my limp head so it falls upon his shoulder, then placing his hand softly on the back of my head, turns it so my hushed lips rest against his neck. "You must drink now."

I don't understand.

I feel his right hand reach down for something at his side – left hand still supporting the lift underneath my thighs – and in the absolute blackness I think I see just the slightest glint as he raises his hand back up toward the meeting of my sleeping kiss. Suddenly, I feel a sharp piece of metal slide flatly between my barely parted lips, then he turns it sideways and I am given a picture in my mind based on the smooth curve of a bladed weapon of some sort; small and razor sharp like a dagger.

"You must trust me," he says.

The edge is inched away from my lips as he burrows it smoothly into the flesh of his own neck. He makes no sound and no movement. His blood begins to run down, falling first onto my guiding cheek and then following its given path into my mouth. He finishes the cut and upon removing the knife, trickling turns to pouring and a steady flood covers most of my face, accumulating quickly on the rest of our sopping clothes and skin as well as seeping down between our conjoined bodies, ending with quiet drips off the bottoms of my hanging feet, steadily pattering on the ground.

I try to scream – to throw myself away from him and away from all of the cascading blood, but I cannot move at all. In a paralyzed state of horror I must endure this. Still completely blind, I struggle to see the events unfolding around me, yet everything appears only the deepest shade of black to my useless eyes; even his thick, sticky blood.

"Empty your mind and listen to me. Hear only my voice, and I shall sing to you through this most difficult part," he whispers amid my silent panic.

Without swallowing or breathing, the blood flows effortlessly past the usual fleshy diversions in my throat, for I cannot use them. My stomach begins to fill and a tingle spreads through my body, climaxing with thousands of miniature explosions as if every nerve in my body is firing tiny cannons through my skin.

"*Wake, awake, for night is flying...*" he sings softly into my ear.

The crisscrossed shapes of tree limbs and enveloping brush appear over one another in the dark like the ribcages of a hundred stilled skeletons as my sight begins to return. Absent of rightful details at first, then as I focus into an ever brightening black and white world.

"The watchmen on the heights are crying..."

A wolf wails in the distance, yet sounds as if he's but a few feet from where we stand. I can hear the softest pitter of floating snowflakes as they strike all that surrounds us. It's as if my hearing has returned tenfold. I hear the winnowing of a bird amidst a distant treetop, an owl making his nighttime calls. Soft as it may be, it cuts through the air and into my ears like a crystal knife.

"Awake, Verity, at last..."

Trembling, I feel it. Shivering not like when I'm cold, but rather as if every internal fraction of my body is beginning to free itself from a cage of death. Every vein and organ inside resonates with my returning life and my mind reconnects wholly again. I begin to kick now and thrash, using every drop of pent up strength in an effort to release myself from this man's embrace. It mustn't be much though, as it seems to be useless in freeing myself, even with my newly strengthened body.

"Midnight hears the welcome voices..."

Gasps now escape my throat, gurgling up trailing blood that has begun to congeal within it. I force myself to speak, only raspy wheezing crackling with thick bubbling liquid is the sound instead that is made. I feel it beginning to clear as I keep straining. My neck feels as if it will burst completely open, muscle fibers popping as I forcefully hunt for my lost voice in still soundless screams.

"And at the thrilling cry rejoices..."

My elusive roar finally escapes, harsh and gravely but quiet at first, then rising – rising into a full shriek. It sounds as if a banshee has repossessed my body, shaking the last of the dead leaves off of their branches and to the ground. Yet even over my wailing, I can still hear him singing to me, his own voice unwavered by my tremendous abandon of self-control.

"Come forth, my virgin, night is past…"

His hand slips up under my thrashing, screaming head and grabs a fistful of hair at the base of my neck, tightening it to a tension I cannot resist against. He guides my head back – back until my spine is fully arched and I'm staring up at the starry sky.

"Your bridegroom comes, awake…"

The falling snow hypnotizes me like a wintry vortex, illuminated by the lunar light of the full moon. My head still back, I fall into it, trying to relax myself for I have no way to fight him. My screaming stopped, I make an attempt to speak, but I cannot feel my tongue. Soft whimpering is the only sound I can make.

He lowers himself to a kneel now, placing me into a sitting position on the ground.

"Your lamps with gladness take…"

Fist still clutching my hair, I feel him pull my bottom lip down gently with the thumb of his other hand, then forcing it to part my teeth, he curls it over my bottom row and begins to slowly open my jaw, gently but with incredible force.

"Hallelujah…"

A cracking sound comes from my mouth, then intense pressure all through my top row of teeth. Two objects fall onto my tongue. I feel them, like tiny pebbles, yet my tongue still lies dead inside my gaping mouth.

"With bridal care..."

He slowly lifts my head and rights it now so we are staring eye to eye. His blood soaked hair brushed back, for the first time now, I can truly see this man and every detail of his face right before my eyes. Handsome and jagged, his features seem carved and weathered, like the statue of a young man that has survived too many storms. I sense something within him, something archaic and warrior-like, as if he could slaughter an entire village of capable men by himself. Yet his eyes remain so very calm. His pupils, dilated black in the darkness with the slightest green ring around them, scan mine with dire compassion. That gaze pushes so deeply into me. No one has ever looked at me this way.

Like I'm all that matters in this world.

"Yourself prepare..." he continues.

Softly, he lays me back once again onto the forest floor. Everything around me is covered in blood, the leaves spattered by it, and pools filled with it which have accumulated in the hollows of the ground. Yet I feel completely peaceful now. Peaceful and very weak. 'Tis if I could sleep for forty days and not be rested.

"To meet the bridegroom who is near."

He spreads his cloak open before me and it flutters in wide ripples at the force of the catching wind. This dark angel, blood covered and serene, climbs over me now, engulfing the surrounding scenery in only darkness once again as his large, graceful body and spread cloak fades everything around me to black.

My mind so completely calmed, I welcome him. I feel his

thoughts within me. I sense no harm, but only his desire for my salvation, for me to be free of pain. Pressing the flesh of his already healed neck back up to my lips again, he needn't make a cut this time. My dead tongue has already begun to move now. I lick the running vein that flows up the side of his neck and as I do, I feel my new teeth — two razor sharp canines that readily accept the invite for more bloodletting.

"Drink until you are free," he says softly.

With bared teeth, I slowly plunge them deep into his neck, which proves much cleaner than a slicing blade. The blood once again flows into my mouth, yet this time it tastes so very sweet. My lips cupped onto his neck and drinking with easy rhythm now, I begin to move my tongue around on his skin. Our embrace gets tighter now, my body warming more and more with each flowing moment that passes.

I feel sleep coming over me more powerfully than ever before.

"Finish your drink and rest now," he whispers. "There's much repose left for you inside this body of mine."

And so I succumb to his words, falling away into my darkened dreams of ecstasy.

He hums softly on as I settle into the stillest calm I've ever known.

***

Awakening, I witness a dark, disorienting place.

Fractured shapes float by and constant muffled sounds wash over my ears. They are quickly lost as I float on through some strange, unknowable chaos. Whether I am now alive or dead, I know not and I care not, for this peaceful purgatory seems all the rest one should ever need.

I look up to see a round white light, abstracting behind flowing ripples that careen all around me in the darkness. Far away, on the other side of my disturbed view, it calls to me, looking so similar to the moon I remember from the skies of my past.

My suspended peace is interrupted by a sudden scrape against my back from something below me and unseen, like a large claw raked down between my shoulder blades – rising from the dark abyss below.

Am I in my body once again? Am I even alive?

It cannot be possible, for my breath has not returned. I can feel my consciousness float endlessly, absolved of bodily existence, yet I feel the urge to reach up toward that fractured light above me. If there is an arm at my side, I try to move it, but I feel nothing. I try to feel where my hand should be, and I raise it to cover my eyes.

The light goes away. Now there's just blackness.

My hand is here; it's in front of my face – I am alive!

I thrust my unseen hand up toward the light. It breaks a surface, into the world beyond distortion – into the cold above...

Into air.

I'm underwater!

Before I can get my legs underneath me, something grabs my hand and snatches me out of my submerged panic, bubbling groans turning to screams as I explode out of the heavy water and into the freezing familiar air, saturated with the numerous and mixing smells of the woods I know as well as my own hands. Skin sensation rushes back to me with the tingle of wet clinging strands of hair which wrap themselves around every part of my face.

I wipe the hair away and open my eyes, gasping for breath as if I was drowning even though I never was.

I hadn't been breathing at all, which is why I thought I was dead. The absence of rhythm from my lungs brings me terror and I begin to tremble. I smell the woods, I feel the cold, I touch my skin as I wrap my covering arms around my breasts.

I feel strangely like a corpse.

I tremble, but I don't shiver. The cold feels almost neutral to me, as if it is a cool evening in late summer, not the approaching winter that brutalizes the village with white death every season.

The woodland sounds resonate sharply clear. I hear the soft but steady trickle of a surrounding stream and look down to see water flowing around my knees, for they are the only part of me still submerged. I feel the rocks under my toes – sharp rocks which would typically be quite painful on my bare feet, but instead seem to provide excellent traction, as if I could grip and spring off of them quickly for an attack.

Why am I thinking this way?

Naked as I stand, I do not have the fear that a young girl would typically feel whilst standing nude in a dark, frigid forest. My body feels different, no longer begging for covering, rather content to be fully expressed for once, as if my bare skin is all I should ever need. This must be how animals feel.

But wait! A hand pulled me from the stream.

Someone else is here.

Looking around, I see no one, yet I suddenly feel that I'm being watched from somewhere near. Completely shameless that I am still naked, I throw my arms away from around my covered breasts and turn to all angles, peering through the darkness like I never have before – in a predatory way.

A rustle in the trees above. I see a shadow, well up high, slink back into the dark covering of leaves which blend seamlessly into the night sky.

Suddenly I catch sight of a large object floating down from the treetops. White and silky, it rides the light winds on its rippled descent toward the bank of the creek I am still standing in, then lands to rest on the ground. I can smell that it's made from recently skinned fur; rabbit fur. I see a hood.

It's a white cloak.

"Why do you watch from afar? Show yourself!" I shout, stepping gracefully across the slippery, stream-smoothed stones, my gliding legs, strong and in perfect gait – my core rigidly tight without effort – making my way to the shore, free of even the slightest imbalances.

Feeling these heightened effects – feeling as I am something more than human, creates this rising sense of superiority, its origins remaining yet unknown to me. For in these woods I should be quite fearful of roaming nighttime man-eaters stalking the forest.

'Tis where the wolves dwell after all.

I think for a moment about them, their glowing eyes and bared teeth. I think of the foraged remains I have witnessed of their victim's carcasses: gnashed flesh lying about in bloody bits, shredded scraps strewn by the ravaging pack.

Then I feel a smile crawl across my lips, for I am absolutely unafraid, even of the wolves. I search inside for fear, but find none.

Snatching up the cloak, I wrap it around myself expecting instant warmth from the coarse, dense fur, yet I feel the same chill as I did whilst standing naked in the creek. Does warmth no longer have effect on my skin? Why do I feel the urge to take it off and be naked again?

My thoughts are interrupted by a low flapping sound coming from above and behind me.

Thud.

I turn to see the dark one from my dreams, kneeling with a bowed head. In a graceful rise, as if he's a knight in a court standing to meet a royal figure, he stands up tall and erect, staring down into my eyes and gripping my soul as he emanates an intensity I have never felt before.

I am certainly not dreaming.

"I am Wilhelm von Immanuel," he says. "And I acquaint myself with highest respect to you." Sweeping his cloak back with his right hand, he places his left hand out toward me and stares at my feet as if in duty.

I hesitantly reach my left hand out toward his, trembling. I feel the cloak nearly slip open; I catch it quickly, clutching it tightly closed with my right hand. But a moment ago, I was so completely comfortable in baring myself to these woods and all its peering eyes. Now I feel my forgotten shy, orphan-girl self come crashing back in the presence of this mysterious man.

He takes my hand in his then kisses it ever so lightly, raising his gaze back up to mine. Our eyes lock as if in an embrace which I could never escape.

"Are you –"

"An angel?" he finishes. "Quite the opposite. Though you say it so often, perhaps it is true."

"I had these visions – these dreams. It was all so confusing," I say.

"I know."

"You were there – I saw you, and yet I cannot remember much. I simply remember your presence."

"Do you remember the blood?" he asks, peering at me quite peculiarly.

"I don't know."

"Close your eyes once more," he says.

I do.

"*Wake, awake, for night is flying…*" he starts to softly sing.

The song begins to immediately bring things rushing back. I see blood now – a knife, my tongue, more blood. A red river of it splashing through my thoughts, carrying fragments of some terrifying dream I must have had and lost upon awakening.

"What is this song?" I ask, opening my eyes. "And why does it bring such terrible images to my mind – images you knew were there?"

He stops singing and looks at me with a grave, but calm look. Like an all-knowing statue, he stands unflinching, seemingly complacent to hold the answers within himself.

The gruesome, senseless pictures still crashing inside of my mind, I anticipate his answer, and yet I get the feeling that he wants me to find the conclusion on my own.

"The song is an old German hymn, *Wachet auf, ruft uns die Stimme*," he replies. "My mother would often sing it to herself at night."

"That may be so, but how then would I have heard it?"

He pauses for just a moment, a slight sadness glazing over his eyes. "Because I sang it to you as you died." His voice is unwavering even at such chilling words, his eyes shimmering with a glint of relief. "You are dead, Verity."

I feel as if I'll faint, yet the sensation passes as quickly as it came, coldly denying me such an escape from those words.

You are dead.

"Fear not, for the worst is over," he says, extending his hand once more. "Come with me now and I shall try to explain everything to you."

You are dead.

You are dead.

In soul-numbing shock, I grab his offered hand and he leads me away to somewhere. He in black and I in white. We move as ghosts together.

***

To be lost is what I have always desired.

To run away — anywhere at all, even into the daunting wilderness — would be quite fine, so long as I could survive long enough to discover just a bit of the world beyond Salem. I had no fear of such an uncertain venture, for I know that the only ones who are afraid to do such a thing are the ones who must say goodbye to someone they love.

But I had no one to keep me here.

Now, wandering about with a strange and unsettling stranger and having been told I've died, I find myself more lost than I ever hoped to be.

Lost perhaps, but dead?

'Tis nonsense to believe I could actually be dead, for I have enough living mind to question such a claim. So mad I must be to believe that, for I can certainly feel nature's wintry breath swirl about the dark patterned trees, coming then going – crawling over my skin before moving on through the night. I can hear the nocturnal sounds of creatures calling out, all with their own purposeful voice. I can smell the potent lingering death; earthy, subtle, but present within the fur of the cloak upon me. I can see all the details of the scenery with new eyes. Eyes that capture every subtlety with a vision I could never before imagine – every tiny movement, every shape too far for normal eyes to notice, I see as if it were near.

And yet, there's something missing inside me now.

There is a hole, one which was not there before. One that I feel has been left by the fragments of my broken soul. A soul which lays in shattered pieces, jaggedly scattered and heavily settled with piercing knives at the bottom of my gut.

These pieces know the truth, for they are the remnants of my life.

How can such be? For if I were dead, my spirit, should I have one, would be gone, carried away on the winds which disappear onward toward uncertain eternity, leaving me to wonder no more. But if I were alive, I would feel my spirit to be whole and complete – like an inner fire, radiating myself onto the world and absorbing the world in return.

Yet I can only wonder still, feeling neither whole, nor gone. Just… hollow.

"I know what confusion must mill your mind," Wilhelm says from beside me, stirring me out of my thoughts and back to this wintry perdition where we walk still. "For that I am dearly sorry."

I stop walking and turn to face him.

"I care not what you say for I cannot be dead," I reply. "I can see your eyes – I see them attempt to peer into my soul. A soul which you say is not there. I hear your voice tell me horrible things, speaking of my death which you claim to have witnessed, and yet, if such were true, I would hear nothing – see nothing. I would feel nothing at all."

"I know grasping such a truth is not without great disbelief," he says, shaking his head slowly side-to-side. "Yet it is the truth, and you must know it to be such, though I know it shall take time." He begins to walk again, leaving me no choice but to follow. "Until then we must move, as not to let the sun rise upon us."

"If I am dead, then why do your eyes look at me as if I have a soul and I am not just a corpse?"

He looks up adoringly at the sky, waving his hand toward it. "Why do we seek out the heavens when all we can see are stars?" He lowers his gaze back down to my eyes to show his sincerity. "Hope remains beyond what we can see. Finding it remains our duty until we can seek no more."

"What are you hoping to find in me?" I say.

"'Tis yet to be found, for your truths have yet to be shown," he replies.

"If I am dead, then my duty is over, is it not?"

"We," he says. "If *we* are dead."

"I beg your pardon?"

"We are dead, Verity. I as well."

After a brief but undoing pause, I completely break.

Sprinting as fast as I possibly can, I crash through stopping branches and tangling briars, but I keep my legs moving, desperately wanting to escape this beseeching madness. Dense clusters of sharp limbs – ones that should tear through my skin and trap me – explode away as if smashed by the breast of a charging stallion. I do not slow a bit; if anything, I pick up speed, evading what I can with unnatural precision, no breath to be caught. My muscles do not tire, my lungs do not heave – how can this be?

I burst through the edge of impenetrable woods, breaking into a clearing – a small, circular patch of earth, surrounded on all sides by the darkened forest from where I just came.

Standing in the middle, as if an appearing ghost, is Wilhelm.

I fall to my knees, absolved of resistance, embracing no escape.

He walks toward where I have fallen and I start to cry, yet no tears appear in my eyes.

"Crying is for the living," he whispers. "There are no tears for us anymore." He kneels in front of me. "Are you ready to become what I have made you?" Placing his palms on both my cheeks with surprising delicacy, I feel his compassion flow through whatever is left of my soul. His eyes tell me that he is loving, however distant and dark he may seem. I knew this before, yet refused to accept it.

"What happens if I say yes?" I ask.

He stands again, looming over my hunched body, then extends his hand. "Shall we find out together?"

CHAPTER TEN

W elcome to my cave," Wilhelm says, walking up to a large protruding boulder crammed into the side of a small rock face. "I call it *Antinomy*."

The cawing of a crow, peering down from a low hanging limb branched out too far from the side of the bluff voices an answer, as if chorusing approval for his hospitable words.

"Antinomy?"

He places his palms against the damp stone, slickly misted by tiny water droplets that had been freed into the air by a nearby waterfall. Then, burying his fingers tightly into the tight seal between the boulder and the hillside, he begins to roll it to his right, the dense minerals cracking apart under his anchored fingertips, crumbling over the stone-slated ground.

"Two opposing truths," he says, halting the stone then turning back around to face me, framed by the blackness of the cavernous hole which the boulder has revealed. "As I am dead, I am also very much alive. This cave is both my home and my tomb."

"How are we dead? 'Tis not possib –"

"Come inside and we shall talk," he says sharply. "For we now have many nights ahead."

Not so evident in the glowing light of the full moon, I realize I can see ever so clearly, even in the absolute darkness. But all is absent of colour.

I thought the night to be especially bright when I could see so well before, yet I am astonished now as my eyes refocus to acquire every fine detail, but only in varying hues of grey. It appears to me that my eyesight has changed, for when there is light, I see in color, but in the darkness, only in blacks and whites.

I scan the room, neatly arranged with a perimeter of artifacts and other unknown objects. In one corner are stacked books and loose paper, in another, the equipment of a soldier: a sheathed sword, chain mail vest, and a medium sized cloth bag with tarnished coins present inside.

"Please sit. There is bedding in the back," he says, gripping the side of the boulder, once again rolling it with incredible strength back in front of the entrance. It is fully dark now, yet he collects what appears to be a large skin of some type, a hide – from a cow perhaps – stretching it tightly across the seals as if to cover even the tiniest penetrations of light that might come through at dawn.

I walk toward the far left corner of the cave, where there is a crude nested gathering of dried leaves and bristly foliage packed tightly together and harnessed in by intricately weaved vines, crisscrossed to barrier the mound from the rest of the room. Lain across the top of it is a large and densely thick fur covering – a bear skin, topping off the makeshift bed with a functional yet powerfully ornamental display. How he could acquire the hides of such powerful beasts? Surely he did not slay a bear with a sword.

"I did just that," he says.

I snap my head toward him, stunned. "How can you –"

"Read your mind?" When you've been as far from anyone for as long as I, a thought can be as loud as a word." He sits at my feet, legs crossed, seemingly relaxed for the first time. "This ability will surely pass as we spend time together. Unless we are connected in the way of the curse. After all, we may very well be the only two of our kind." He looks sad for a moment, and then his eyes smile a bit toward me. "Can you hear my thoughts?"

I stare into his eyes, focusing, straining to hear what it is he thinks of.

"No, I cannot hear anything."

He smiles wide and stares deeply into me.

I must look quite taken aback at this, because he comes back to his original form, removing the smile and resuming his stony expression.

I can only stare back at him. This Wilhelm, intimidating as he may be, speaks to me in a way no one ever has before.

"My apologies, 'tis been many years since I have conversed with anyone, yet I owe you a promised explanation in regards to the serious nature of things." He stands, no longer in any way relaxed, instantly transformed back into a man of formal attention. He paces slowly back and forth as if a castle sentry, attentively guarding a post.

"Who are you?" I ask almost sympathetically. "Where did

you come from? How did you end up here? Why did you bring me?"

His face displays a man collecting thoughts. Pacing still, he removes a piece of twine from his pocket and ties his wild hair back behind his head, making himself look regal in one transition. "My name is Wilhelm von Immanuel, son of Katherina and Johannes Immanuel," he says softly, but with an edge of militarism in his voice. "I was born in the small town of Werder an der Havel in the Margraviate of Brandenburg under rule of Elector Joachim Frederick."

"You are from across the world?" I ask.

"Yes, I am of German descent and traveled here by a merchant ship."

"But what of your accent? 'Tis hardly foreign sounding at all."

"I've been listening to many cultures of people speak for many years now," he says. "Rather effortless it is to absorb such common dialect when one hears it every day."

"You speak English then, but your native is German?"

"Yes, and French, and even some Latin as well."

"And your dress – you appear how I imagine soldiers to look."

"Not a soldier." he says with a glint of shame in his eyes.

"Despite what you say, it is quite clear to me that you are a living man, so what is all of this talk of death?"

"I was once a man, as you were becoming a woman," he says, gazing off into some unknown place. "We aren't either of those any longer."

"How is that so?"

He removes his heavy cloak, neatly folding it and dropping it to the floor, then begins unlacing his black patterned doublet. Opening it and exposing his chest, I see a large scar run across the striated ripples of his dense muscles, straight down the center of his breast. "Because I too died," he says.

"'Tis but a scar," I reply. "Surely you survived, for you stand here in front of me now."

"I certainly did not," he says. "Lain across an altar and impaled by a dagger in the winter of 1629, I was twenty-seven years old when my life was taken – only to be replaced with this abiding curse."

"1629? But that means –"

"Born in 1602," he states. "I have remained in this world for forty three years, yet have wandered it alone after my natural death for the past sixteen." He looks at the floor as if gravely ashamed. "*Nachtzehrer,*" he says in a language other than mine.

"I'm sorry?" I reply.

He looks back up at me, slightly surprised. "A German word for things which should never be." He turns his back to me now, as if he has something terrible to say and cannot face me. "Have you never heard of the vampire? Surely with all the blood-drained animals in your village, such speakings must have arisen amongst the people."

"I know of vampires," I say. "I also know that such things are lore."

"Then we are nothing more than fables," he replies, turning back to face me with a dire look in his eyes.

"What you mean to say then, is that we – we're vampires?" I do not even believe my own words.

"Yes," he says. "We are the living dead – *sumus lamia.*"

"Such things do not exist!"

"I'm sorry, Verity. I know it is a dark truth to accept, yet truth it is. That's why I was killed. I asked for this curse. I needed time and I needed power, and now I've given it all to you."

Impossibility floods me. I feel like I'm trapped in a nightmare, though I know 'tis all happening. The stories we were told as children, of the blood-drinking undead. It was all real. I am real. "No – no. Take me home right this instant!"

"You have no home anymore. None but this tomb we must share together now."

I dash off of the bed faster than I thought possible – right to the sword propped against the wall, then draw it on him with equal speed. "This ends now," I say with a tremble to my voice. "Move the stone and release me. I've heard quite enough insanity from you."

He opens his arms, inviting me to make a move. "Shall you drink of my blood again if you spill it?" he asks, moving in slow steps forward.

"I shall drink nothing," I say, not daring to avert my eyes.

He steps slowly, but assuredly toward me. "Oh, but you enjoyed it…"

"I care not what you have to say," I snap. "Open the door."

"But of course," he says, waving his hand coyly. "How silly of me to think you could remember your own resurrection. Moving between living trances and dying dreams leaves a broken memory which holds nothing to recall once it has passed."

He remains but a few inches from the tip of the blade.

"Halt yourself."

"You drank of my blood as if it was the last drink you would ever receive," he says. "You savored every bit, slaying an eternal thirst that I have beset upon you in necessity of bringing you back to a life you begged for."

"Speak no more. Move the boulder."

"Courteous as it may be to do so, I shall not, for you need to realize your new strength by rolling it away yourself," he says. "'Tis much easier than it looks for one of our kind." He continues to move slowly toward me.

"Now. Do it now," I say.

"Though I fear 'tis not a good idea," he replies. "The sun has surely risen, and we needn't be scorched before we complete our work."

"I shall not ask you again!" I yell, the blade now pressing onto his chest, quivering my hands with tension.

Before I can say another word, he moves onto the tip, piercing his skin with a quick pop and slides himself into it without even the slightest hesitation in his movement or a sound from his lips. "I knew it would come to this." He slides all the way up the blade, a trickle of blood escaping out the exiting wound and down his back, lightly dripping onto the floor.

I stare only at his eyes, knowing he has reached the guard of the sword only when I feel the bump of the handle press into my own chest.

His hands wrap quite softly around mine. "I have no reason to lie to you, Verity," he whispers with real sincerity in his voice. "'Tis what we are, and we must embrace it."

Shaking, the words escape my mouth without any thought behind them. "Why?"

Wilhelm steps back, guiding the sword from my hand and in a swift, experienced swipe. He pulls the blood-sheened blade from himself, admires it for a moment, then brings his eyes back to mine. "So that we may save ourselves."

***

I'd spent many of my human nights crying into my palms, my skin moist with hot breath and tears. It had become almost routine. I would sob for awhile in my own little darkness and then after a bit, I would slowly relax. My back would fall more softly as my lungs found normal breath again and when 'twas all over, I would always feel much better. But for hours now, I've been sitting in the same fashion, only now everything is cold. There are no tears and no breath, only dry cold, dark palms which do nothing to ease my dread.

"Are you not what you wished to become?" he asks softly, easing the prevailing silence.

"Regretfully, I am just that," I reply, deciding my silence is doing nothing to calm me so I may as well speak. "I've spent many a night staring out into the woods hoping to catch a glimpse of you, dreaming of how I may be whisked away into your unknown world one day."

"To be freed from your detested Puritan life," he says.

"Yes, to be free," I confirm. "Yet now I sit here, a demonic monster – trapped inside this cave like a common animal with no one to save me."

"I saved you," he says. "You cried out for vengeance and I answered your call."

"You saved my body, but what have you done to my soul?" My thoughts sit on that last word. "When I was human still, I thought nothing of any afterlife, but now that I've been resurrected into something else…"

"I freed it from the prison of mortality and now you have the gift of forever."

"I wish I had been granted death instead," I reply. "Then I would be completely free."

"Then why didn't you just kill yourself before this all happened?" he asks, sliding next to me, sitting together on the stone floor. "Because you weren't ready. You still have your desire for life. I gave you a new one. Maybe I am your guardian angel after all."

"We are heretical creatures Wilhelm, not angels."

"You know nothing of what you speak," he says, leaning his head back against the wall, staring out into a sky that isn't there. "You have not lived enough yet. You have not seen the evil that swirls within men. True it is that we now drink blood to survive, yet do these mortals not drink their savior's blood in hopes of preserving their spiritual survival as well?"

"'Tis only their desire for righteousness that compels such tradition," I say.

He stabs me with a stare. "If intention defines sin, then we are all vampires, my dear."

I look to the floor, afraid to meet his eyes. I understand his points, yet I cannot rid myself of the feeling that we are not just unnatural, but unnatural and condemned, walking in the footsteps of darkness if only by our immortal nature alone.

"Shedding one's blood in sacrifice for others is not a concept solely begot by their supposed savior," he says. "One must only go to war to see mortal men do the same. Then you shall witness a truthful cause of sacrifice unfold into a false following of those disillusioned enough to partake."

"So what then is your cause, Wilhelm?"

"To find spiritual truth," he replies with absolute conviction. "Scouring the earth studying the texts of various cultures: this has been my life thus far. 'Tis much too easy for someone who has only seen one way of life to follow the common religious pattern. Much harder, yet nobler it is to question in hopes of finding…"

"In hopes of finding what?"

He looks at me for a moment with a quiet question in his eyes. "Verity."

There washes between us an eerie wave of silence. "Is that why you saved me?" I say with frustration. "You believe I am your truth?"

"Your name would suggest the possibility of such a claim."

"Even if I was, you destroyed that possibility when you cursed me."

"For many years now, I have picked at the corpses of cultures like a raven, living outside of society, waiting patiently to find another scrap," he says. "Pecking at bits of texts and knowledge, I never gave up the hope that I would one day taste the truth."

"So it may be, but what does your spiritual journey have to do with saving me?"

"Throughout those years, I have only felt meaningless – empty and cold, as you do now."

I shift anxiously, aware of that eternal ill feeling once more.

"Until that night," he says. "That night I heard your screams, something inside me was rekindled once again, and I felt all of its warmth." He takes my hand within his. "I knew I had to save you, for it was spoken to me within my soul."

For the first time since my death, I feel my emptiness replaced by a glimmer of peace, delivered solely by his touch. I feel my shoulders begin to relax, as we exist only within each other's eyes for a moment. This man truly saved my life. Sure, 'tis different now, but he transformed me. He brought me back to life and gave me all I had ever wanted. He fulfilled what I shouted for as those men murdered me. He gave me another life. Another chance.

He made my wish come true.

Raising my hand to his face, I place my palm against his cheek as his arms stay tightly to his sides. My touch seems to have frozen him still. He looks past me, so I place both hands on his cold cheeks now, and I feel a slightest hint of warmth rise within them. I right his eyes to mine. This man, he has done more for me than anyone ever has. How ungrateful to him I've been. "I'm sorry, Wilhelm. You're right. I asked for this."

Our eyes burn together for a moment. Looking into the face of my beautiful savior, far from the world, we burn alone.

He pulls away. Once again standing in the middle of the room, he has reacquired the rigid soldier stance of before, only a look of shame upon his face.

"What is the matter?" I say.

"We are no longer limited by the boundaries of time," he says. "With that, I cannot be so careless with our new life together, for we only have each other now, so we must carefully guard our hearts."

I throw my head into my hands. "That's all I've ever heard," I say. "Spoken far too often are those words, always telling me to guard my heart – *guard it from impurities, guard it from lust, guard it from dark thoughts,* they preach." I stand up and face him, feeling myself to be his equal now. "You are not Satan. I do not fear you and so you should not fear me."

"'Tis not about fear. I shall first be your mentor and your protector."

"Quite funny coming from a man who stripped me naked and left me under the current of a stream in the woods."

"There was purpose for that," he says. "You needed the acclimation process. The darkness, the cold water, it helps you transition more peacefully into your new existence."

"And what of my nakedness?"

He looks at the ground once again. "'Twas necessary to wash the blood from your body."

"My immortal baptism," I say. "Commenced by you?"

"I suppose it was," he replies, rubbing the sleeve of his shirt.

"There is a test in Salem, you know – in order to find witches," I say. "They bind the hands and feet of the accused then throw them out into the river. If they float they are guilty, if they sink, they were innocent, but drown to death anyway. It makes me wonder how many of them wished to have been able to lie at the bottom in rest as I did, waiting for the crowd to disperse so that they might emerge from the dark depths and into a new life. A life far away from the broken one they lived before."

I step toward him, catching behind his large upper arms with my small, but purposeful hands. "I am innocent – innocent and alive – all because of you, Wilhelm." I stare deeply into his uncertain eyes. "I'm starting to find peace now with this gift you have given me – hard as it may be to do. I can promise that while I may struggle with these terms of existence, I shall never be ungrateful for your saving compassion. You offered me a second life."

He starts to speak, but my fingertip pauses his lips.

"Thank you."

***

The days dawn and dusk. The rising sun greets the land like a radiant salvation covering the landscape of nightmares bred in the night. Then just as soon as it comes, it disappears once more, leaving the world as prey to the desires of darkness again. Fear of the unknown nights keep the people in their homes huddled around their fires – their own little suns which banish the demons from their lives.

However, we all must submit to the dark, for it is the only pathway of rest. It is in this way that the very process of life forces us to face our demons each night in our own souls. In the places that fires cannot glow.

Yet now, as I am a vampire, the days are meaningless – 'tis when the mortals mill about their lives like cattle, hardly living at all. Where once I feared the night and all its uncertainty, I now realize the day is nothing more than a loud blinding over the true beauty of stillness.

Wilhelm revealed the night to me in proper introduction, and it is magnificent.

I find myself now not wanting to sleep at all, and yet Wilhelm insists I must in order to acquire my full transitional strength. He tells me that sleep is not necessary, but in the early stages, your mind has yet to realize 'tisn't necessary anymore, and so it hangs on to the familiar comforts of rest.

I spent my first full day in his lair, sleeping away the sun. Wilhelm had vowed to stay by my side so I would feel safer as everything still feels scary and often he says "We have very unpleasant dreams" in the beginning of our new state.

None such things occurred for me however, and while I actually remember nothing at all from my dreams, I do remember clearly of what happened before I drifted away, and this interests me much more.

Wilhelm had taken a seat on the floor bedside, and while he knew I was awake, he did little more than stare vacantly toward the opposite wall which remained covered by his collection of artifacts. I had thought it odd that impatience had not settled on him as he sat there silently, waiting for me to fall asleep. But after a pondering, I realized that impatience does not plague the vampire, for when one becomes immortal, time no longer matters and with such revelations the mortal emotions that derive from the idea of time dissolve.

However, when he believed I was sleeping, he moved toward the far side of the room, and after rummaging through that which I could not see, he reclaimed his spot on the floor, his back against the wall and a leather-bound journal of some type resting against his knees.

It was then he cut his wrist with a stealthily drawn dagger.

Bleeding out droplets into a small glass ink vial from a clean and even slice, he appeared concentrated, as if not to let one droplet stray from his chosen path. After he had filled the vial, he pressed his other palm to the wound for a moment and then removed it, and I could see that the cut had closed.

Then he opened his journal and began to write with a blood dipped quill.

Curiosity naturally grabbed me. *What was he writing? Did it speak of his past?* I wanted to know more about him. He chose me after all to save, to accompany on this "journey of spiritual truth" that he speaks of. Now that my fears are over, I find myself hopelessly interested in who he really is.

Those eyes, so deeply set and hidden back behind his falling strands like a forest of shadowy trees, remain so inescapable. So penetrating and sincere his gaze is, I swore his journal would catch fire at any moment.

I can see him as more than a stranger now, for not only has he shared bits of his past and his motivations with me, but rather I simply feel safe. He is not a monster – *we* are not monsters, or demons or any other hellish things that the church would surely sentence us to be. For even a vampiric curse has a place in God's world if he so allows it.

But I don't believe anyone is watching.

Besides, I see nothing of the sort. I see only a deeply contemplative man, withdrawn and unsure, losing himself slowly on this journey of finding himself. I do not know him well, and yet it is what I know to be the truth, perhaps from somewhere deep in the connected places of our minds.

I can feel the surge of his discontented pain, and I know not how to help him find peace, for I am lost with him now in his uncertainty. I am frightened. I fear the loss of meaning. I fear that immortality steals it from us, for things seem to be only meaningful when the certainty of death haunts every corner of our lives. What shall happen once I reach an age beyond that of a human life? Shall I end up hopeless and empty like Wilhelm?

Or can we reclaim our stolen meaning through togetherness – through love?

These senseless romanticisms are certainly not rational, but I cannot ignore the growing warmth I feel inside my cold cavernous self, this heat that floods the remnants of my soul when I look at him. I cannot help but feel that there is more between us – that we are merely in the early stages together. And yet we are meant to be here, away from the known world, trapped in timeless exploration together by fate.

I never even believed in fate.

But I never believed in vampires either.

Yet here I lie in this tomb with the lingering taste of blood still in my mouth, inhabiting a cave with the only other one of my kind that I know of. I have become what I did not believe to be real and how curious it is that the village I have since left is inhabited by hundreds of people who believe angels are real and have never even seen one, let alone become one themselves.

With my new eyes, I can see the blindness of my former mortality.

Now I feel my body weakening, as if by patterned remembrance, my thoughts beginning to tire, and I feel that sleep is coming for me. I look once more at Wilhelm and I can almost see the invisible broken pieces lying around him as he writes. The shattered picture makes no sense and I feel that he will only ever share with me the shards of his former life. Oh, but I wish to see his whole portrait.

The matters of my desire must wait. For it is time to rest, and my eyes are getting heavy even as my lids are nearly closed. In the darkness as I drift into sleep, I am carried away as Wilhelm's scent floods my curious mind with mysterious dreams.

CHAPTER ELEVEN

Many things awaken us. The call of a rooster, the low rumble of wagon wheels spinning over grinding gravel which cracks and pops under heavy loads. The clip-clop of horses making morning rounds through the village. The laughter of those delighted with a cornmeal breakfast around a fire. The sunlight's warm rays, pouring through the window pane and across the bed sheets in striped patterns of golden glow. Mostly though, we awaken to our own internal noise. The dissipating vapor of a passing dream, leaving our minds as we come into awareness. The cold morning air in our lungs as we exhale a visible breath. Our heartbeat, slow and steady – awakening us to a rhythmic pulse that has been an awakening reminder since birth. Consistency in the most purest form of internal harmony – the sincerest indicator of life.

And now I have no heartbeat, no heaving breath. All is still and silent within me.

Upon awakening, I have a pause now – one in which I am forced to find myself in a few moments of panic. My mind remains confused each night, for it has no internal signal of life anymore, leaving it to desperately grasp for a shred of reality.

As I awaken, I realize what my clearest sense of living is: hunger.

Painfully empty, I feel my stomach lurching for food – for blood. A cramping runs through me, my muscles tense and hardly usable, my legs like dead fallen trees. I open my eyes as I writhe in the bed and I see Wilhelm leap to his feet and rush to the bedside. He quickly slashes his wrist open with the dagger.

"Here, Verity. Drink now," he says.

Without any hesitation, I throw my lips around his wound and begin sucking out every bit I can, for I feel so incredibly drained. As if I'm dying all over again.

The effects are nearly immediate. I can feel my strength rushing back to me now. With a strong sense of hunger still lingering, I know the effects of that small amount of blood are temporary and a feast must be attained.

No sooner does that thought cross my mind, Wilhelm pulls his wrist from my mouth. "That's enough now. Time to find you something more."

I step out from under the bed covers and quickly realize I'm naked. Wilhelm has turned away as he begins to roll the large stone away from the entrance. I stand there for a moment and hesitate to clothe myself with the white cloak. Not only do I feel free and so comfortable now in my own skin, but part of me wants him to see me this way, for we are no longer humans bound by custom and shameful tradition. We are pure, and we should be like nature again perhaps, free from human woven threads.

Yet for his sake, I snatch up the cloak and cover myself once again.

We emerge out of one darkness and into another. The sun has become nothing more than a memory to me now and I wonder if someday I shall forget it entirely.

Wilhelm grasps my upper arm and guides me as I take my first few steps.

"How are you feeling?" he asks.

I look up at him and smile. "Fine." I mean to say more, but 'tis all that would come.

"I remember how difficult it is," he says. "That terrible feeling in your body, ill and starved. Such a horrible hunger comes upon us in the beginning. While your body is finishing the changes, you will require much nourishment, and when you awaken you will be very weak."

The open air brings with it the trailing scent of animals: mice under the snow, still rabbits trying not to be seen, the eyes of birds above, watching for predators and prey alike. The woods possess its own system of blood; each track in the snow has become a vein running to a source from which to feed. My senses overwhelmed now by the crisscrossing possibilities of paths to follow, I stop dead and begin scanning from side to side, attempting to get hooked by the strongest scent.

"To your left," he says.

Searching for a moment, I smell only a faint trail. Then suddenly I've got it. It hits me like a hook in my brain, dragging me toward the source.

Without hesitation I begin moving. Trotting at first, then running faster, moving effortlessly through the heavy snow which would slow many creatures down. But my driving starvation is enough to propel me through it. My feet barely penetrate the powdered surface as I glide like a ghost.

"Stop," Wilhelm whispers sharply. "Your eyes – use them now. Forget your hunger for a moment."

I was so focused that I had forgotten Wilhelm was behind me, but I freeze at his voice. Silently, I take an observing position, peering into the dense forest around me in an attempt to find movement of the blood source.

"Up ahead," he whispers in my ear, sending the first shiver down my spine since my transformation.

His body so close to mine, I almost forget my purpose for a moment. If it was not for the insatiable hunger within, I may have turned to kiss him. He trembles something deep within me. Something I've never felt before.

"Be steady, smooth, until you are close enough to hear the heartbeat," he says quietly. "Then strike."

I move, my eyes so focused on a large grey rabbit up ahead that the woods around me fall away like a dream. 'Tis if I'm staring into a hole with nothing but the rabbit on the other side and all I must do is reach down, snatch it, and commence my drinking.

The snow has powdered a light dusting over its fur, creating a brilliant camouflage when compounded with its motionlessness. I hardly believe I would have ever noticed it at all if it had not been for its scent and my newly sharpened eyes.

Now I realize full well what has happened. Wilhelm saved me as prey and turned me into predator.

I was the rabbit, wandering aimlessly with no real direction, simply trying to not get hurt by the wolves around me while I went about my life. Yet at my most vulnerable moment, when I was to be consumed by a clan of these voracious beasts under the cover of night, something far more powerful emerged from the darkness and freed me. The torch-wielding wolves showed their cowardice and scattered when challenged by a true predator – a solitary one who does not need a torch to banish the darkness, but becomes the darkness. Feared by those who cling to the comforts of light.

Now ahead of me, the rabbit looks away, and I see my chance to strike.

I take three large bounds then leap into the air above it. As I'm falling I can hear its heart beating clearly: fast paced, but steady, not rising one bit, for it doesn't know that death is descending.

Upon landing, everything comes together at once. My feet slam on either side of it, creating two walled barriers in the snow, and simultaneously my hands shoot down and snatch it up, feeling a slight crack when my palms land on its back.

I know it has been mortally wounded, and as I turn my hand over and face its belly up toward me, I feel no struggle from it at all, just a slight twitching as its left foot attempts to kick in very short and weak bursts. Perhaps its spine has been broken.

Without thinking, I go to finish it off with my gaping mouth and bared fangs.

"Wait." Wilhelm says, appearing beside me. "You must first show your respect to the animal, for it is a sacrifice to you."

"How so, a prayer?" I reply.

"No," he says. "A silent meditation of gratitude, for you are consuming it so you may live on. This rabbit brings to you the gift of his own life and you must cherish it entirely."

I stare at the helpless, wide-eyed rabbit for a moment, and I suppress my hunger enough to realize the irony of the situation. When I was a rabbit myself, faced with killing my own kind at the stump behind the orphanage, I had nearly gotten sick at the thought of butchering it for food and instead released it. Now I cannot wait to tear into it, for I am no longer its kind. I am above – a predator now, simply trying to eat.

"Close your eyes."

I do.

"Now, as you take this moment of necessary appreciation, concentrate on how you and the rabbit are connected, both existing in this world together. As it serves a purpose, so do you. The transition of dying to live is not a separate event; it is all one. As the rabbit dies, it becomes a part of you. 'Tis a cycle of unending sustenance among all things in which we must always remember and be appreciative of."

The hunger still radiating inside me becomes numbed a bit by this calming of my mind. I understand now. Like the predators of the church who attempted to consume me so they might sustain themselves as well. Everything is connected, yet loses this touch in a world of appearances.

"Only when we reflect this way, do we begin to remember our rooted connections to everything." He closes in behind me, his chest against my back bringing the chill into me once again. "Now you may eat."

As I lower my fangs to its neck, our eyes fall side by side, and I am surprised by the lack of any fear. It looks peaceful. Even as I begin draining its blood and the heartbeat fades to nothing, the transition of death seems as if 'twas supposed to happen.

As if the rabbit was aware and fine with such a thing. As if even in death, he understood Wilhelm's philosophy better than I.

I finish drinking and set the body back on the ground. I scoop out a hole for it in the snow and lay it inside, repacking the snow over it for a quick, wintry burial. As I rise, I catch Wilhelm's eyes transfixed on my chest. My cloak has fallen open, and tricklings of blood run down my breasts, staining the edges of the white rabbit fur red.

He catches my notice and quickly rights himself, looking toward the sky. "We shall go into the village now while they sleep to find you some proper clothes, for yours are stained and constructed with crudity."

I let out a sigh. I do not want to cover myself anymore, yet I silently agree to his wishes. "And then what shall we do?" I ask.

"We shall begin our studies together, for you have much to catch up on, and *we* still have much to learn," he says with a heavy voice. "But first we shall go back to the cave and assess what else we need, for we must keep our village visits sparse." He looks back down the path we took.

"I also would like to retrieve my journal" I say.

"We shall," he says, still looking forward.

And then we walk slowly together, back toward our lair, our tomb, our home.

***

A date I know not of, 1645

Before today, my writings which are enclosed in this book have been only recordings of my dreams, nothing more. Now I feel I shall write whatever I see fit, as my life is now seemingly a dream, only I am awakened to it.

Wilhelm has opened my eyes.

For the past few weeks he and I have barely left the cave, absorbed in studying the ancient texts that he has gathered throughout his travels across Europe and to the new world. Wondrous and exotic writings they are, from places I have never heard of. It is quite spectacular to think of how much world there is away from here, across vast seas and unending landscapes, for I looked just into the woods beyond the orphanage as if it was another world itself. Now I wish to travel to these places, to see the world beyond here. We have read these texts together and I take great delight in learning from the stories and the history which surrounds them.

He has told me that what Salem's ministry propagates is not truth, – that they hide so much from us all and lie when they must. He tells me that one must only find the origin of the lies to discover the inception of their creation.

He and I began with studying history and while it was hard to believe at first, he has shown me the true origin of this Puritanical faith, a constructed religion in which my former people follow unquestioningly to their graves. This was hardest for me to understand not intellectually, but spiritually rather, for it is all I've been told my whole life and 'twas the core of myself that could not let go of such inherent tradition. Even whilst my mind knew the fallacies and my soul was haunted by the truth that would never be told to us. But I knew no other spiritual alternative, and most importantly, Wilhelm says, I didn't know the world's history. Such enlightening revelations bring wonder to me, for I believe this world would be so very different if all people sought for the truths that Wilhelm has spent his existence attempting to find. I am so fortunate to be privileged with this knowledge, yet sad that such wisdom must be a privilege, as everyone should know the truth.

Without it, we are but living lies.

I do not know what shall come to be in regards to continued spiritual searching. Wilhelm seems concerned in the tradition of witches, for if witches are here, he believes they may be able to provide us with more knowledge about spiritual existence and afterlife.

He is a man of many concerns, his plight so visible in his eyes it makes me shamed to think of my only concern as of now.

When all of this is done, what shall he and I become?

***

Somewhere in my past, there is a lost moment when I knew 'twas wrong. I cannot define the moment or remember when it floated into me, all I know to be true is that there came a time I stopped believing. That's not to say I didn't believe in *anything*, but rather I felt that the truth was likely so very, very far from what was preached in the village. I felt it was far more fantastical than dread and damnation, that there had to be real love and magic somewhere beyond this fearful life. For a long time I was terrified of thinking such a way, but the night I died, I was saved from ever trembling at the feet of my beliefs again.

Now, in sitting with the man who saved me, I wait with intention, longing to absorb even more from him, each of his words a key unlocking secret parts of me that I've hidden for so long.

"What wonders you the most?" he asks.

Sitting cross-legged with him on the floor in front of the many books stacked in the corner of our home, I am enamored by how much knowledge there could be, settled in the corner of a cave. "What have they all taught you?"

"They've taught me to keep searching," he replies. "To never settle for an easy ending."

"What do you mean?"

"This is a duty. We have a power now to learn beyond the bounds of mortality. This is our gift, and we must not waste it, but search beyond death and never stop until we have learned all we possibly can about spirituality, curses, witches, worship and everything else we possibly can." He pauses for a moment, then a look of uncertainty comes to his eyes. "And then we must share it. But before we ever get there, we must repel the urge to stop looking when we find an agreeable answer. That is most important."

I think back to all those people I would see in service on Sundays, bowing their heads and forcing their fierce prayers into whispers delivered to nothing. They never asked if they were wrong. They never searched for more. In their falsity they remained with fleeting moments of happiness and a lifetime of fear.

"What books do you have?" I ask.

He smiles silently for a moment, presumably overwhelmed. "Well, – I have many. There is... a copy of *The Bhagavad Gita*, *The lost Gnostic Gospels*, some translated excerpts from *The*

Egyptian Book of the Dead, The Qur'an, The Codex Regius and many, many more. But fear not, Verity. We have many years to read them all."

"I've never heard of those."

"I know," he says. "They will never teach these books in the colonies."

"Well, they should have many more books than they do," I say. "Especially important ones such as these."

"There is no use for them," he replies. "Why teach of any history other than Puritan history? 'Tis far easier to continue ignorance than 'tis to answer questions."

"What are they about?"

"They are dead stories," he says. "About Gods from long ago. Gods who died with their people."

"Gods can't die."

"Ah, but they can," he says. "They are the myths that bring hopes and dreams and comforts to their people. They are the ones who children and elders alike cry to in silent prayer and rejoice to in celebrations. They watched over their children and gave rest to their dead. They carried their people through the ages, and then they died with them."

"But God's presence remains strong in Salem and elsewhere," I reply.

"And one day that will change," he says. "Salem's God will die like the rest."

"You're sure of this?" I ask.

"I am sure of this," he says. "Everything changes."

"How long will Christianity last?"

"'Tis hard to say. Christianity started many centuries ago

during the great Roman Empire and their influence was so profound."

"The Romans?"

"Yes, by Emperor Constantine." He pushes his hair back from his face and his prominent eyes burn with passion as he shares his knowledge with me. "He required the strength of a unified empire and to create one, he felt it best to unify the people at their core, so he unified their beliefs. Christianity was just one of many religions in the empire and was ultimately decided by the emperor to become the official religion of the empire."

"But the empire was so long ago…"

"Their great coliseum stands today," he says, "and 'tis only stone. Stories can be shared and passed down and far outlive stones. Structures are of great importance to emperors, but most important are the structures of the mind. 'Tis why Constantine focused on this matter and made great religious change with his council of bishops."

"Council?"

"The Council of Nicaea."

"And had this council not occurred –"

"The people of Salem may be praying to Mithra instead," he says with a coy smile. "Or maybe no one." He sits back and folds his hands together into a single fist. "See, people are not created in God's image. Gods are created in ours. *We* write the stories."

"You know so much," I reply, longing to hear it all. "I cannot wait to embark on this adventure with you. To travel and learn all we can. To become the few who can change this world and speak the truth."

Moon-sparkled oceans and towering dark mountains form themselves in my mind and I think of all the far-away places we will go together. The limitless world is ours to seek and we will pull truth out from the shadows of every dark corner of this earth. We will weave them together to learn more than has ever been learned before. We will gain mastery over our lives and over our ends. They say the truth sets us free, but the truth is not our master. We shall set the truth free, but most importantly, we shall set *ourselves* free.

I come back to Wilhelm and he's staring at me again in that serious way of his.

"What are you thinking about?" he asks.

"I want to learn of witches," is what I say.

But then my heart whispers. "*Us.*"

CHAPTER TWELVE

N ight is approaching," Wilhelm states with mission in his voice. "We must go now and begin our search for the documents of the church – the ones which pertain to witches."

"How can you be sure they exist?" I ask, still questioning his certainty.

"There were many rumors in my old land about the new colonies," he replies. "Far too many suffered a fate at the burning stake. So many of them fled, offering assistance to the church in order to acquire amnesty for themselves."

"And you believe one came here, to Salem?"

"Of that I can't be sure, but I know the church at least keeps historical archives – ones which document all coven associations."

"Coven?"

"Their gathering."

"And why would the church associate with heretics?"

"They hold many answers," he replies. "Those who own true wisdom – they own the world and its people," He looks at me seriously, "but not us."

We leave the cave, and my skin tingles as the last light of dusk falls behind the tree line, leaving the world just dark enough for us to safely enter. After a short walk, we reach the edge of the forest, the glowing windows from afar penetrate the blackness appearing like stars beyond the sliver shadow trunks of the trees before us.

"We must be careful," he says. "They musn't know we are in their village."

The town ahead appears so far away. A meaningless memory to me now, and one which hardly ever passes through my mind. Yet the slow burning bitterness within has never quite left my murdered heart. It still simmers in the bottom of my being. Still begging my hands for revenge.

The only part of that life I miss is Hope. I still think of her probably more often than I should. I remember her rubbing my hair at night. She would never stop until I was asleep. I remember how her bravery in the face of the ministry led her to such a tragic end while I was spared for showing the same. Mostly though, I try to remember the fun times we spent together as girls. Carefree, we would race to the edge of these woods – the ones which I now call my home, daring one another to go beyond the forested line at dusk when the shadows had begun to sweep the sun away.

Not now, I tell myself. I cannot dwell on such things, for Wilhelm and I have a mission tonight and I cannot disappoint him. This is why he saved me. To have a partner for his journey.

For *our* journey.

"Keep your senses sharp," he says. "We shall be quick and

silent. Once in the meetinghouse, we will be safe to search, for no one shall be there before sunrise."

In following him, I move forward hastily, patterning my movements after his and admiring his tactility in navigating the last bit of wooded terrain.

We break clear together into the open and I feel as if the whole village can see me standing out in the exposing air. I know they are all fast asleep by now, resting their mortal bodies weakened by the human labor needs of the day. The meetinghouse appears high above the houses before us – not far from where we stand. We head toward it, staying in the available shadows whenever possible.

Passing these houses reminds me how I once longed to have a family. I wished to know my mother, to find out what happened to her and why she abandoned me there in that horrible place.

The Bridge to Salvation Orphanage looms off to my right like a nightmare waiting to be revisited. Existing as an ominous reminder of the horrible human life I once endured, a miserable childhood which shouldn't be lived by anyone. I wish it to be burned. I wonder if Goodmother even cried when she was told of my death?

Perhaps I will burn it once we're done here.

We are almost to the meetinghouse when Wilhelm stops, pulling me in close to his side. "Sometimes they may stay to work late into the night, so let us be careful as we enter."

I nod to him in obeying silence.

Moving together toward the back of the building, we stay close to the oak exterior so as to blend in with the dark. I look to Wilhelm for each direction given by his body and I simply follow.

It has been quite some time since I have seen this Wilhelm, for in our life he is far more reserved and relaxed now that he trusts me as his own and lets his guard down a bit more with each passing night. Now however, his diligence takes precedence and he becomes the formidable soldier he once was all over again. His eyes have taken on the look of a predator, glowing ever so slightly as his intense gaze scans every possible problem around us.

"Stay here for a moment," he says. "I shall enter and once inside, I'll open the window above you."

I nod again.

Wilhelm disappears silently around the corner and I crouch into the hedges which adorn either side of the back door. As I wait, I can smell the odor of boiling potatoes penetrating the normally scentless air cooking in a house fairly near. What once would water my mouth now makes me feel pungently ill, for my tastes have changed.

In the distance, I can hear the soft wails of a baby crying out into the night and I quickly realize how hungry I've become. In all of our studying we haven't foraged even a drop today. How terrible of I to think this way, and yet I can't shake the urge...

Creak.

Just above me the window has slid open and Wilhelm extends a hand down. He knows I could easily scale the wall myself but remains gentlemanly just the same. I grasp his powerful arm and he hoists me up and through the slim opening.

The smell of the meetinghouse brings back the horrible memories of a lifetime spent attending this place. The minister's voice haunts my mind. I hear the weak chants of the disillusioned villagers seeking salvation, their eyes saying they are willing to do anything for it. I can see them all; hear the nervous rustles which indicate they are truly, truly afraid. They tremble for the invisible, and remain blissfully unaware of the true threats in the world. For true monsters lurk in God's house tonight.

Never having ventured past the nave before, the shadowed hallways appear spooky, even to a night dweller like myself. But Wilhelm shows no hesitation, no caution in his step – only intention. For 'tis but I that keeps memories of this place, not him, and 'tis those memories which send me chills as I move through them.

Approaching the end of a hallway which I had never before seen, we arrive at a heavy oaken door, built it seems to behold a dragon within. If there was anything worth protecting from view, this was surely the room to do so. Alas, this door was not built to repel the immortal strength of the cursed or the determination of Wilhelm.

Scanning over the cold dense wood for a moment with his flat palms, he seems to find a weakness. Digging his fingers into the side with the hinges, he begins to push. The door creaks and groans behind his force and then it explodes open, the hinges left hanging on the frame alone. Before the broken door can crash onto the floor, he catches it.

We have been rewarded with beautiful silence for a mission nearly complete.

He lays the door slowly onto the ground and I enter the room, looking all around at the immensity of documents shelved in untouched organization. I run my fingers along the rows like blades through dust, collecting the film on my fingertips.

"There is so much in here," I say, overwhelmed by the immensity of volumes stacked to the ceiling. "How will we ever find the ones we seek?"

"We have much time yet," he replies, barely acknowledging me, presumably attempting to find a starting point in which to begin his search. Then with a mind far away he whispers to himself, "I will find it."

In quiet possession, he begins crawling about the room like a spider spinning a web with his mind – consuming each title he sees with his voracious eyes as they all surrender.

I follow his lead, attempting to make sense of the language which adorns the covers of these books – a language which I do not understand. "Wilhelm, I cannot read any of them. 'Tisn't English."

"Latin," he says sharply. "Look for words such as *venefica, lamia, incantatrix, saga...* I presume those will be the ones pertaining to witches."

Focusing closely on the titles, I try my best to make sense of the foreign writing.

Commentaria Seniorum...

No, that cannot be the right one.

I pick up speed, words flying by my eyes. I try to place each one, keeping in mind all the while the ones which Wilhelm had said to find.

Missiones Ecclesiae...

No.

Interfectores Ministerium...

No.

Wait, something's wrong in here. I feel it.

I quickly look up to Wilhelm, who has turned away from the books and is facing the open doorway. He snarls like a wolf preparing for a kill.

Whipping around completely, I see what has transpired.

A young man stands in the doorway holding the service staff like a weapon he's never used. Frozen in place, speechless and trembling all over, it seems he's already aware that he has stumbled upon his own death.

I remember him.

The boy is Thomas, from Grace's wedding.

I sense his fleeing thoughts: he's going to try and run. Before I can move, Wilhelm has flown across the room and snatched the boy up, throwing him to the floor in the center of the archives.

"Why are you here?" Wilhelm demands.

"I – I – uh..." Thomas stutters.

"Speak!"

I can do nothing but watch, for I know Wilhelm may kill him at any moment. I fear greatly for anyone who stands in his way as his mission means far more than anything else. Even more than the life of this boy.

"I clean the church, sir," he finally says in a voice high with fear. "I was in the hallway sweeping and saw the door open. N – nothing more. I fell asleep earlier in a pew. I had to finish. I didn't mean to be here so late."

Wilhelm's eyes are blazing with rage now. I know he never expected this. "Tell me what you know of this room, of the documents in here."

"I know nothing. I am but a church hand, sir," he replies, still sprawled about the floor, clearly too afraid to stand.

"Surely you've heard rumors."

"Only that such a room existed – never have I heard anything with regard to the contents or been granted access."

Wilhelm stares at him unblinkingly, pondering how much truth there is in his fearful voice.

Wondering whether to murder him now.

"I'll tell no one of tonight, sir," he says in a begging tone. "I shall even fix the door before sunrise if you wish."

Awaiting Wilhelm's next move, I am caught in a rush of anticipation – a strange desire to see him unleash his power on this boy. Such weak creatures these humans are, groveling to be spared at the feet of one much stronger than them.

I cannot believe I was ever one of them.

Wilhelm steps forward slowly – an executioner – one serious step after the next, boots like thunder clouds carrying an inescapable storm. Then he kneels in front of the trembling rabbit in peasant boy clothes.

"Be gone," he whispers solemnly with a hiss of boiling restraint. "Tell no one of tonight or the demons of the forest shall find you."

The boy rises slowly, still unsure whether he's actually been granted pardon, and as he backs away, his trembling seems to grow. He runs down the hallway, then the back door flies open and slams shut behind him as he takes off into the cold night.

"Why did you spare him?" I ask with a surprising tone of disappointment.

"Why should I kill him?" he replies. "Will it help us find our spiritual answers? No. Such an act only takes us farther from salvation, not closer."

"He will expose us. We cannot risk it."

"I hardly believe so, for I know the characteristics of men and that boy wants to forget tonight ever happened, not revisit it."

Perhaps it was hunger or maybe cursed desire, but I wanted to see Wilhelm tear the boy to pieces. I wanted to see his dark blood pour about this room – this hidden heart of the church, beating each day with the pulses of false belief. I wanted to drink of him, lick his blood off this holy floor...

"They are not expendable, Verity," he scolds. "We cannot murder humans simply because of opportunity. We must take the higher path, even if it presents us more difficulty. We must be gentle with the world."

I look at him with challenging eyes. I want to argue, but not now. Not while we race the dawning sun. Instead, I lower my head in submission as he turns his back to me, resuming his search.

The feeling that we let our own incrimination run out the door sits heavy on my mind though, for if he were to tell the village, they would likely arrange a gathering of willing hunters; ones who would scour the woods with torches until they found our home. While I don't believe they could stop us, we would never have a life of peace again. Not while Wilhelm needs answers that only the church can provide.

As much as I hate this village, we still need Salem – if only just a bit longer.

An idea crosses my mind.

"Let me go," I say. "I shall follow him – make sure he goes back to his home, not stopping to wake anyone with news of our meetinghouse breach."

"Fine then," he replies, hardly looking up from the mountainous volumes before him. "You'd better hurry and be back well before sunrise. We cannot risk it."

"I know."

No sooner do I speak and I'm already at the end of the hallway, slivering my way back through the window still ajar from our entry. As soon as my feet touch the cold ground, I start off, using every scent I have along the way.

I can smell him still – see the ridges of his footprints which had dug the ground in fearful haste. Moving so fast now, I care not if anyone were to see me because they would never catch me anyway. I would be simply a ghost to them – haunting their village and serving as a reminder of the numerous people who have been slain unjustly.

My only concern is finding Thomas.

Within what feels like a moment, I see him up ahead walking, perhaps fatigued by his nerves and hard running. He must have thought he was beyond danger. They always do.

I follow closely enough almost to touch him yet he does not realize I'm even there. For over his hard panting and lumbering, heavy human footsteps crunching on the ground, surely any sound in the night would be drowned out. Especially my mostly silent stalking.

I know not where he lives, but I watch his movements closely, anticipating his intentions. If he diverts toward any other home…

Walking alone in the middle of the lane, villager's houses on either side, he must feel slightly comforted – slightly safe now in the center-most part of town. He hasn't an idea that an impending death follows him from above, crossing the treetops, waiting for any signal to fall upon him in a bloody finale to this night.

He stops, breathless.

Placing his hands upon his knees, his face falls toward the ground. His head hangs tired, little beads of sweat glistening upon the ends of disheveled hair strands which stick about his face.

Then muffled voices from a house to our left and firelight glowing from a window tells the story of a family still awake even in the late hours.

He lifts his head, looking toward it. The front door swings open and a large, unrecognizable man steps outside in an irritated haste, slamming the door shut behind him. He begins walking around the back of the house.

The boy looks toward him with questioning eyes. I can sense his thoughts.

Don't do it.

He must be thinking he's safe – *far from the monsters I am now*, he believes as he spins quickly to alert the man from the house.

As he opens his mouth to speak of events, I hit him with all my bodily force, spearing my claws into his mouth and fish hooking his cheeks as we both slam to the ground.

He looks up at me wide-eyed, blood now pouring from the tracks of open flesh on his face. "Help! Somebody come out!"

His screams crash into the air and so grabbing the back of his neck, I slam my hand over his mouth and nose, pressing his desperate cries back down his throat with all of the strength I have.

His eyes, brimming with terror, beg for his life as he writhes, straining to make a sound that someone will hear. Even as I crush my palm against the front of his teeth, his shrill voice finds a way through and I see a light from an open door – the man's door.

This has to stop.

I grip my claws into the flesh on either side of his neck, then slowly I puncture it, burying my fingers behind the cartilage of his throat. I crush it all. Blood leaks past my hands and only the slightest wheeze rasps out of him. He shudders for but a moment with falling eyes, then he fades away.

As I stand in the shadows of the night, a gust of wind flies by me and on it, I hear the carried pleas of pardon that this boy never got to say. For a moment I feel a bit of remorse for killing him, but like the autumn wind itself, quickly moving by, all things pass.

Then as I begin moving to find some hanging clothes devoid of soaked blood, I pass a window that brings warm, fragile humanity back into my dead heart.

Framed and glowing in warm candlelight, Purity sleeps in her illumined bed, peachy and golden she seems the embodiment of warmth. Only a glass pane away, but far enough from all of the night's cold horror, she is a world away from me.

Approaching her window in the glowing blue moonlight, I feel much like a ghost out here alone, watching. She's so peaceful, so very human, and it saddens me how much I've missed her.

Far away from my old life, I had nearly accepted that I would surely never see her again, for 'twas to be only Wilhelm and I alone in our new path together. Yet part of me longs to speak with her once more, for I had only just touched the surface of a friendship I felt could be a deep and everlasting one before I was taken into the woods to face my death.

Against all of my better judgment, I slowly press on the pane and it creaks softly, for 'tis very loose. I notice my hand has left blood streaks on it, so I kneel to wash my hands in the snow. The blood, still warm and wet, cleans away easily, leaving no traces behind. I rise back to the window and push it out of its spot with relative ease then I climb inside, needing to be near Purity. Once in, I right the pane back into the frame, for the frigid air need not disturb her.

I glide over to her bedside, her human aroma completely intoxicates me as I approach. I couldn't turn back now even if I wanted to. Her scent swirling about and warm blood draws me dangerously close to her throat now. I place my hands behind my back, gripping them tightly so as not to touch her. I want to devour her and it feels like both hunger and lust. This warm blooded princess beckons every part of me to her.

I lower my open mouth to her throat. I want to taste of her, to let her flow onto my tongue and drink of her, but I know she would soon die.

Like a flower picked from the roots, I would own her, but

only for a short time. For she would soon wither away like all picked flowers.

The tips of my fangs now press gently on her skin. My tongue moves forward. I slide my fangs harder into her neck. She moans softly, invitingly…

No! You cannot do this!

Suddenly, she raises her arms and begins to wrap them around me in embrace, like two enclosing shackles from which there is no escape. *Get back, Verity!*

I fall away from her, retreating into the shadows in the far corner of the room, away from the touch of the candlelight. Away from her.

A moment of silence passes, then she stirs.

"Who's there?" she asks with a shaking voice.

I remain frozen, resisting the urge to respond or to run back to her. Her attraction is too powerful. 'Tisn't safe for me to be near her.

Nothing that powerful is safe, for it owns us more and more with each step closer.

"I know there is someone else in this room," she says, strangely fearless. "Just show yourself."

Knowing there is no way out without killing another tonight, I decide to just step forward from the shadows.

"Verity?" she says with evident surprise. "But – I thought… they said you were dead."

"Never mind that," I reply. "I came back."

"I must be dreaming. What happened? The blood – there's blood all about your clothes!"

"'Tisn't a dream," I reply, "for I came here to see you."

"Ghost. Y – you're a ghost," she stammers.

"Hardly," I reply. "But I am here to do some haunting in Salem."I almost smile.

She looks at me, now coming to terms. I see her fear slowly slipping away. She is accepting the situation now.

"Purity, I haven't any time to explain myself. I need your help – some clothes, if you have any you can spare, I need them."

"Of course," she says, throwing the blankets back and rising from her bed. Her white sleeping gown flowing behind her as moves, she appears a white angel in the divine candlelight – so pristine I nearly hold a breath that isn't there.

She quickly rummages through some folded linens that are stacked neatly in the corner of the room, then grabs a set and moves toward me, holding them out in presentation. "Will these do?"

"Yes," I reply. "Thank you." And as I take them from her, our hands brush and I think of tossing the clothes aside and grabbing her instead.

Why do I feel so *strongly* for her?

These feelings I have eclipse the ones for Wilhelm. When I'm with her, I feel imprisoned by attraction. For a moment I feel bad, but the moment is overshadowed by this perfect creature before me.

Purity is simply a different kind of power.

"I must go now," I say with dread in my voice, having lost track of time completely and knowing Wilhelm has not. "I shall return soon though and then I will explain everything to you, I promise."

Her large glowing eyes burn with a hundred questions, yet she settles for none, accepting my promise of return. "I'll be waiting."

She steps forward into my shadows and embraces me in a way that makes me want to stay forever. Then she pulls away and steps back into the candlelight, and I remove the pane once again and slip back into the cold, dark, silent world that is mine.

As I remove my crimson stained clothes in the moonlight, for a moment I feel low. I feel as if I'm nothing more than a murderous animal, undeserving of my life because I took it from another.

Then a thought of solace comes over me: *even the most compassionate of creatures will kill when their livelihood is threatened.*

And these threats are ever present, disguising themselves in many forms. Sometimes they murder and flog and control, evidently powerful like Barrowe. Sometimes they plead, they cry and scream, seemingly powerless like the church boy. All of them equally dangerous except for one.

For the most dangerous of all is the temptation of an angel.

***

Before I return to the church, I know Wilhelm has left it. I know he has contented himself with a midnight watchtower among the trees above me. I catch his scent carried on the naked air as all other smells have been boarded up in their houses or their barns until the morning.

"Why were you gone so long?" he asks among a leafy rustle as he emerges from a small cluster of pines behind the church, still surprising me just a bit.

"The boy traveled far and he traveled slowly," I reply. "I had to follow the whole way to be sure."

"And he made it home?" he asks.

"Aye," I reply, cringing at my own response – one in which I always used with Goodmother. One in which she knew I was certainly hiding a lie.

He stares at me for a moment, seemingly forever. "Your clothes?" he asks.

I look down at my new white sleeping gown. In the moonlight, it almost gleams as if 'tis newly made. The dainty fabric dances around my body in the wind and I quickly think of something to say. "The robe was cumbersome. I saw this hanging on a line and I thought it to be more appropriate. I like it much better. I may have died, but I'm still a girl who doesn't wish to look dreadful all of the time. I stole these too." I hold out the clothes Purity had given me, hoping he'd be pacified with the idea of seeing me in a normal outfit.

He just stares at me.

Can he still read my mind or has that passed?

"Did you find the texts?" I ask, breaking the incriminating silence.

"I found mostly nothing, but took some volumes of historical records," he replies, "a few of which may have something written on witches."

"I'm sorry, Wilhelm," I say. "Shall we be leaving then, or shall we search more?"

"Home for tonight. Perhaps we may find something tomorrow."

I'm aware of the shift from the nights' empty chill to the

morning's dew-scented air as we begin our journey back to the cave. The smell of watery pine implies our need to walk with haste as to avoid the breaking dawn which shall be upon the land in a short while. A prevailing silence between us as we walk is quite characteristic whenever Wilhelm is bothered by matters. I've quickly learned not to question him during these times, but I fear if I say nothing, I will blurt out my crime in a fit of boiling guilt come undone.

Not guilt for the killing, but rather my betrayal to him.

"Tell me of the witches," I say, quite sincerely curious. Suddenly, I remember the book Purity had given me, the emerald one of witch history. I think of asking him to get it, but decide against it.

He marches forward, diligent and stern-faced, gritting his teeth with frustration for not finding what 'tis we sought. "What do you wish to know?"

"Anything at all," I reply as lightly as possible. "Have you ever met one before?"

"I have," he says. "Back home, in a cathedral where their covens would commence in secrecy."

"How were you allowed in there?"

"I wasn't," he replies with darkness in his tone. "I was sent there to kill them all."

"Kill them?" I say in such shock as to remove my thoughts from my own crime. "But if you were to kill them all... is that what we're here to do?"

"No. Not here. Here we are to find one for our assistance in learning of our spiritual place. Back when I was hunting them, I was paid. I was a mercenary hired by the Catholic

Church to eliminate all witches who were assisting the Protestants with their reformation. The Volarc witches they were called."

"Volarc?" I repeat, curious as can be about such a special lineage of beings.

"Yes," he says, "and the Ulrica witches are the others – the ones whom I was hired by."

"So you must know much of them both," I say, quickly digging for more.

"Well…" he starts, searching for how to speak of these matters with me, for there is much terror I'm sure he carries still from these times. "The Volarc are the white witches – the unbinding ones who serve the church, acting as mediators between the spiritual and the living world. They have been called many things before. Centuries ago, they were the Druidesses, the witches of the ancient Celts. They presided over religious ceremonies, assisted with spiritual mediation – even politics and treaties weren't beyond their influence.

"And so they are all good then, only seeking to help?"

"For the most part," he says. "But the others, the Ulrica witches, are quite destructive and evil, only looking to further benefit themselves through any means of coercion and manipulation. They are never above using black magic and the like to achieve their dark desires. They descend from the Seeresses that practiced within the Germanic tribes, the ones who assimilated into Roman rule by selling themselves out to assist in conquest for protection within the empire. They betrayed their people and they will do whatever they must to preserve their status and power. So many of them stayed within the secret ranks of the Catholic Church, helping to vanquish the Protestants whom began to rise prominently in Europe. They assisted in persecutions and torture and other terrible things to benefit the stranglehold of the Catholic Church."

"So how then did *you* come to work for them?" I ask, regretful as such a charged question escapes my lips.

"I was much different then, Verity," he says with evident remorse showing behind his iron demeanor. "I was filled with pain and was looking to level it upon those working to do well. I felt more satisfaction in destroying the beautiful things which were beginning to emerge. I knew nothing of peace, nor did I care to assist in its creation."

"But how did the Ulrica find you in the first place?"

His marching stops and he turns to face me with emanating loss in his deep, darkened eyes. "I fell in love with one of them."

Whatever fragments left of my heart crumble away, leaving a hole now where something was before, something I wasn't aware of until it just left me. I can hardly stand my rising jealousy and the questions exploding from my mind. *Who was this girl? Why do I care so much? Do I love him? Does he feel anything for me? Why won't he ever explain himself? Why won't he ever show anything?*

And what then of Purity?

The attraction I feel for her resonates from a different place, one of pure desire. I can hardly pull myself away from her whenever she is near. I find myself hypnotized by her beauty, wishing I could embrace her and never let go. I never thought I'd feel that way about a woman.

Is that how he felt for her?

"What happened to her?" I ask, selfishly hoping she died a horrible death.

"I don't know," he says, hardly hiding his pain. "One day I went to meet her and she never showed again. I used to be so resentful of this, but time heals. Now I believe that people pass through our lives for reasons. When they're meant to be there, sometimes they'll come back – other times not. Either way, all will be fine."

Wilhelm's implication of destiny brings back questions I used to ponder often when I was lonely and fearful of how short my human life would likely be. We were all told in church of God's plans. Our fate was predicted and yet we were instructed to work in service of God and the colony, to prosper and live a noble life. All the while the Church participated with witches, never forthcoming to the people with true wisdom and instead maintaining that a life of toil was one we should all be thankful for.

'Tis what made me question the existence of God at all. For why would he fate us all with lives full of chores, hardships, sickness, sadness, and hunger until we finally die? The all-powerful could certainly have granted good people a more desirable life, if they so earned it in the fashions which we were told to conduct ourselves.

Does he believe in destiny? Does he think we have an unwavering fated path we must travel? I suppose such an idea brings the most peace to an immortal. I don't think he would proclaim to know, but the fire in his eyes is evidence to me that he is quite determined to find out.

With my passions roaring furiously inside me – both for Wilhelm and Purity – I can hardly think of anything else. Life and death cease to matter when you are lost in the struggle of love, and I shall need to figure out this unexpected situation soon.

"What was her name?" I ask, pushing my jealousy away as best I can.

"Semira," he says with a voice layered so heavily with sadness, I fear he may decide to stow away on a charter ship back to Germany tonight in hopes of finding her again.

"'Tis a beautiful name."

He says nothing more.

We are nearly back to the lair when the morning birds awaken and greet us with sprightly chirps, and it makes me long for the pleasantries of the sunshine, warming the land and filling all with life-bearing light. Yet while all else livens up under the waking sky of nourishing gold, I must retire to the unchanging darkness.

Oh, how I miss the sun.

"We may have to travel to another colony," he says.

The words shock me. "What for?" I reply, glancing toward him to gauge his seriousness. I can hardly bear the thought of never seeing Purity again after tonight. I am spellbound by her.

We mustn't leave.

"If there are no texts to be found here, no witch residing in Salem Village, we must travel to a new area."

"But you said they are here," I reply with a voice pitched high with worry "We need but some more time and we will surely –"

"We were seen tonight, Verity," he snaps, cutting me short. "Our presence is known – if only by one boy, that is still one too many."

I want to scream my confession now, tell him that the boy is dead, tell him of how I tore his throat open for us so we may remain together – our life unchallenged by the human world, unspoken by any who wish to expose us and our home in the woods.

"Where would we go then?"

"A Quaker village perhaps," he says as if he's thought of this before. "Far enough they are from here so as not to have heard word of us from Salem. Tensions keep talk between the communities rare."

"We cannot run, Wilhelm. Our home is here."

"What then shall we do?" he asks with cutting words. "Shall we rot away in the woods for all of eternity and watch the seasons pass forever, never learning anything more of our spiritual fates? Or do you suppose we march into Salem and demand the texts – threaten to kill all who assist in hiding them from us and presumably slaughter the whole village? We cannot become monsters."

I face away from him, letting my head fall and my vision fade out of focus as the ground dims away and my nervous thoughts come forward.

"If we cannot find the texts…" I say slowly, thinking carefully about my next words, "then we find the witch."

"The witch?"

"Yes," I say, surprising myself even. "We find the witch and we kidnap her – force her to tell us where the texts are, releasing her only once we have them all."

"We don't even know if a witch is here," he says. "And even if one is, we cannot just steal someone as our captive."

"But what of me? Did you not steal me away from the village?"

"That was different."

"Perhaps it was, but I should believe 'tis better than running."

"Enough with this!" he snarls, his eyes ablaze and directed like arrows awaiting a slight touch to launch into my soul. "We shall not speak on this anymore tonight."

I know 'tis the failure of the night which breeds the hostility in him, and yet to appease him for the betterment of our circumstances, I silence myself.

Then as if in perfect concluding rhythm with our walking debate, our sudden cease of discussion is finalized with our arrival back to our lair. It appears different this morning as we break through the dense parts of the forest and into the little cleared patch around the mouth of the entrance. Different because it could be one of the last days we ever spend here.

For our futures are always so very uncertain.

CHAPTER THIRTEEN

For a day now Wilhelm has brooded over his books like a beast over a kill. Hungry for meat, but finding only bones to chew. The ominous silence between us is sour and I think it best not to speak to him, if for the simple reason that I don't want to become the recipient of the same contemptuous dissatisfaction that has overtaken his face as he pours over books which seem to be helping him none too much.

I know that his moodiness arises from passion. A dedicated man such as he can be quite ornery and 'tis only because he has devoted his energies to something that he believes can change the circumstances of the world. I am not mad at him for that 'tall. I believe in his cause and I have become excited myself to be on this journey with him while we explore every path of spirituality, known and unknown. I am thankful to search for all I have ever wondered about.

My only wish is that for just one night, he will look into my eyes and forget about reading any pages in any books and see only me. I want him to crave me like he craves the trails that he walks in his books. But he cannot touch those, and I wish he'd touch me for just a moment like the world didn't matter. There is no life or death in the moments I desire, but this new life that has been born between us is not lacking in time and I know the love I need will be abundant once this seeking has ceased. That is why I must help him with this journey. When all is done, maybe we shall inherit each other's hearts.

I look up to him and he hasn't moved. A thought creeps in about how silent and stone-like he's been since we've returned and almost on cue, he closes the book he was reading with obvious irritation.

I feel quite uncomfortable as I watch him shift about.

I need to go. I need to get out of here. I wish to see Purity again. 'Tis terrible of me – I'm sure of it – but the way she looked at me was like firelight warming something inside me, begging me to stay with her.

"It is dark again; I'm going for a walk." My voice cuts the silence far louder than I expected.

I'm not surprised when he doesn't look up, content to continue his scanning of book spines. I wonder for a moment if I even bring any purpose to his life. I never see him soft. He never smiles at me.

"Why?"

"Because it is still nightfall and you are still reading."

"That's fine," he replies. "Show care."

For a moment I feel like shooting back something snide in return, but I settle for just leaving. I move across the room, hoping he'll stop me and bring me back to him, but as I open the door, step outside and seal it shut, a flicker of excitement in my heart creeps up when the cave stone seals.

That little flicker of dishonesty.

I push the thought aside as I walk through the night. How repetitive. Darkness and trees, darkness and trees. I move among darkness and trees and nothing more in this gloomy midnight life. For a while I felt so free, and now I feel sometimes more of a prisoner to the dark than I do freed by it. When I'm not moving through a silent night, I am sitting in a tomb. This is not the life I dreamed about leaving Salem for.

Unfamiliar smells bring me back from my mind's complaints and I stop to look around. I fear I've gotten myself lost. I had started off in the right direction, but somewhere along the walk I must've strayed at the fault of my thoughts.

The cold aroma in the air is so powerful. Powerful and floral...

I walk a bit farther toward an area of the forest that is dense, full of tangles and clumped pines. I move through it with difficulty, then I finally break through.

I'm standing in the most magnificent flower garden one could ever dream of, and it's all covered by ice.

The sudden frosts must have preserved the flowers under crystallized dew before they had a chance to wilt, creating the most alluring sight I've ever seen. Like a fairytale palace of color and ice, the regal spot seems it was destined to be found.

I pull myself from it, knowing I have only a short while to visit Purity, but I take in all of the scent I can as I move back through the barrier of pines and into the dark monotony of the barren forest, reeling from the surprise of happening upon something so hidden and beautiful. It reminds me that Wilhelm and I will soon be doing this together. We will be uncovering all of the untouched and unspoken treasures of the world. What a wonderful thought and yet it brings me sadness as well, for I know we will have to leave here and I won't ever see Purity again.

I stop walking and look up to the sky.

Guilt grips my heart. I want to turn around and go back to Wilhelm to save myself from the pain of secrecy. I know I shouldn't be going to her tonight, but 'tis almost as if something even more powerful is pulling me to her and I cannot free myself from the beckoning of my heart.

I should go back.

Go back.

***

Purity's still awake when I arrive, her smile at the window gleaming out at me before I'm hardly even close enough to notice her. She must've stayed up thinking about me, watching for me to come back.

I cannot get Wilhelm to speak or even look at me when we are together in the cave, and she stays up all night waiting for me to return. I hardly feel as guilty now as when I left.

I see the flicker of moving torch lights in the distance to my left and down the road I hear voices moving hastily away. I know what the stirring is about.

She opens the window for me and I climb inside.

"Tell me honestly," she says before I can speak. "Did you kill that boy?"

"Yes."

"Why, Verity? Why would you *do* that?"

"I had no choice," I say. "He saw us. He was going to speak of us to the town. I couldn't let that happen."

"Us?' she asks.

I hadn't yet told her of Wilhelm. "I mean *me*. He saw me and was going to scream about it to everyone! The churchmen would surely look for me and I wouldn't be able to ever come back."

"You shouldn't have done that," she says. "You shouldn't have. He was a *boy*."

"He was told what would happen should he say anything."

"You did this for me?" she says.

In my mind, I know 'twas not the case, but in keeping with the honour she is most noticeably expressing to me, I say "Yes."

She hugs me tightly.

"I must remain here in Salem for a while more," I say to her. "I cannot be forced to leave yet. We would never see each other again."

The pain of selfishness pierces my soul. How terrible is it of me to lust for her while also keeping feelings for Wilhelm. He gave me my life back and I'm here with her. What is wrong with me?

But he and I are immortal and when you have forever, forgiveness must come eventually. Besides, I need to be here. I need to feel this and know her once again. Wilhelm gave me new life, but not before my old one was stolen from me and I miss Purity so much. We were on the verge of something special and to leave this all behind…

She separates us and stares into my eyes. "I've missed you."

"But I've only been gone for a few hours."

"I know."

My hand is in hers and we are moving toward her bed. She guides me down and I sit next to her. "I just cannot believe you killed him."I say nothing.

"What does it feel like?"

"Silence," I say.

"Silence?"

"Yes," I reply "I stole his scream and made him sleep forever. I suppose it was kind of a beautiful way to die."

"Do you think it hurt?"

"No."

She looks at me with longing eyes. Her hand slips over top of mine and she slides nearer to me. While she is only mortal, I feel strangely overpowered by her still. The little Puritan girl in me remembers how she made me feel before and these feelings remain beyond my new form. I try to speak, but my words are chained to stones. I cannot pull them from my mouth. I cannot move.

She's closer now.

She's going to kiss me.

Footsteps thud on the porch outside. *Who's here?*

Purity pulls back and jumps up.

Boom, Boom, Boom!

"Miss Lightfoot!" a man's voice yells from outside. "Miss Lightfoot, open your door please!"

"You must go," she says. "Go now!"

I bound to the window. "I shall see you soon, Purity. Soon. I promise."

Out the window, running to the edge of the woods, far from view, I turn now and face her house. The torches are abundant and human chatter disturbs the air.

And so tonight, the witch hunt for me begins.

***

The whole walk home is haunted by the ghost of guilt following closely behind me. Slipping through the trees, I feel it come close and bristle my neck with memories of all that I shouldn't have done. Visiting Purity was probably wrong of me, but more so now I'm worried about that boy I murdered. People will be looking for us now. They will likely scour these woods, and I fear they may find us. Should I tell Wilhelm of it? What then would he think of me? He would likely tell me to leave and I would forever hate myself for speaking when I shouldn't have. We would lose this magical future that we hold, and I cannot risk that loss. I believe it best to never speak of this, to try and forget and maybe one day, centuries from now, I will.

Maybe secrets can hide the truth, but perhaps only when they're buried deep enough.

I arrive to our home and I notice the boulder is rolled aside a bit. The quiet crackle of frost under my feet must be alerting because Wilhelm comes out to greet me, lively and warm and smiling. Gone is the sorrow, the defeat that shone from his aura when I left him to his reading. I feel myself smile too.

"I'm so glad you're back," he says. "I've found something."

He glides to me and takes my hand faster than I can respond. Leading me inside, I notice all of the books and loose papers that had been scattered about when I left have been neatly stacked back into the corner, except for – one loose sheet of paper that he picks up carefully and holds close to his body. He smiles again. There is so much life in his eyes.

"This is what I've been looking for," he says. "This means we are close."

The joy I feel doesn't overshadow the fear I have that we will be found. I know it would likely be best for us to go far away from here. They will be looking for us now and 'twill likely only take a few days for them to discover our home.

"Read it to me," I say.

He straightens the paper out and focuses intently on the words, for they are likely faded and worn. "It's a document," he says, "an agreement between a lawyer named John Winthrop and a church representative in England named John Gaule. Dated 1629, it states that for the amount of a thousand pounds, Gaule was to recruit a new council witch from the Germanic lands to come to the colonies and serve as a guide for the establishment of the new church in Salem."

"And he did?" I ask. "It says he did, yes?"

"It does." He turns the document over, showing the back. "It has been officially sealed as a completed agreement. Mister Gaule's witch likely remains here in Salem. We could stay here and seek it out, but the better option would be to find John Gaule, for he knows the identity of Salem's witch, but also has a wealth of connections to the covens of England. I believe that everything we need to know on witches can be found through him."

"Wilhelm, that's wonderful!" My arms are around him and

I lay my head on his chest for a moment, letting his smell come into me. I step back and in one full motion, sweep all my hair back from my face. "This means we would have to travel to England then."

"Yes," he replies, "'tis almost the end of the month, so there is probably at least one ship leaving tonight that we could take."

Tonight? I feel my expression shift beyond my control, falling somewhere between surprise and sadness with maybe a bit of fear.

"This troubles you?" he asks. "Why do you want to stay here close to Salem? We have no reason to at the moment, for greater things await us than this tiny village. I thought you wanted a new life with worldly experiences?"

My guilt creeps back and it finds its way to my eyes. I fear he sees what I keep hidden inside. "I just… I feel 'tis our home." My feet pace about and I look at the floor. "I want to travel, I want to explore, but part of me…" I pause and look at him. "Part of me will always want to stay. This is where I was born, and 'twas where I died and sometimes I feel if I were to leave, that little bit left inside of me – the bit that feels human – will be gone forever."

He looks toward the ceiling peculiarly, as if trying to remember the feeling of "home" that eluded him so very long ago. "I understand. I suppose I had forgotten of sentiments." He finds my eyes again and his are rekindled by humanity, so evident now from a man that sometimes I find quite cold and far away. "Verity, I know this life we have now… it can become dreary and boring and I know you must become bewildered by all of the research and silences, the time spent alone and the times when I become upset or quiet. I know it must dampen you and for that I am very sorry."

Looking into him, I remain silent. Silent and surprised by his apologies.

"I want to take you somewhere," he says. "A short traveling... tonight."

My hands tremble at my sides. "To where?"

"Boston," he replies. "Roughly forty miles away, we would be there well before sunrise."

Surprise creeps into my voice. "Boston?"

"Yes," he replies. "We can go tonight and I can show you the harbour, the ocean, maybe even take you on a ship. When you get there, you can decide then if you'd like to leave this place."

"I don't know what to say."

"Say nothing. Just walk with me."

***

The sea-salted air of Boston is even colder than back home. I hold Wilhelm's arm tightly and we move as two villagers freely through the main street. There are so many others out here tonight, for it is a bustling city even when the moon is high.

We brush past a stumbling couple who smells of liquor, laughing loudly and dancing with exaggerated twirls and kicks as they pass. I watch their sinful hands under the cover of dark, finding each other in places they shouldn't touch. A man peers at us from behind his spectacles; his boots echo off the stone with heavy clops as he marches toward us. His eyes catch mine and my soul freezes. He smiles forcibly and tight-lipped and I return the favor as he passes and goes on his way.

I hadn't thought how strange I would feel being around humans this way again. I tremble and cannot stop my eyes from darting around at everyone as we walk, waiting for them to catch on to who we are. He remains so calm and must sense my inner struggle because he pulls his arm out from my grasp and puts it around my shoulders, pulling me in close as we walk.

"They do not know us," he whispers. "Enjoy the city."

I walk assuredly with him until we reach a bend in the road and round the corner toward an archway shone in lantern light. We stop before a building with a bustling inside and windows aglow, standing alone at the corner of the streets. The sign above us reads: BEAL'S INN.

I wrap his arm tightly with both of mine. "Are we going in there?"

"Yes," he replies. "Don't be afraid of people. I think it will be good for us to go and make some conversation. We need to reconnect to the world sometimes before we fall too far away from it."

I force a smile, telling myself that this is good for us. I think about it so often but in my mind, it never scares me. All of the work we do is not only in benefit of ourselves, but of the people as well. I just can't release my fears that they will sense all of our secrets, that they will find us out and ruin our hidden life.

He moves me gently forward. "Come now."

Wilhelm grabs the salt-rusted handle and pushes open the

dampened grey wooden door. It swings back and the life of the room floods over me. A heavy warmth from body heat and stove fire slams into my skin, the low roar of conversations and hearty laughing drowns my ears, and the pungency of spices and ale floods my nose and covers my tongue, the seasoned air masking the smell of blood that pumps through the room.

He keeps me moving and leads me toward a small round table with empty stools in the back corner. Everything here is so bright and colourful. Pictures are hung about the walls as well as shipping pieces and other symbols of Boston. My eyes revel in the beauty of the light. I glance over to Wilhelm and he has never looked so surreal. For the first time ever, I notice his eyes are of a cool green, set deeply into his face framed by falling hair of auburn brown.

He sits down and while staring at him, I also try to find myself into a stool, but when I reach to pull it toward me, my hand knocks something rather large onto the floor. I look down and see 'tis a leather bag of some sort. Its flap has fallen open from its clasp and some paperwork spills halfway out of it.

"Worry not, my dear. 'Tis rubbish anyway!" I hear a man shout in a distinctly English accent. I look back up toward the tavern bar as the source of the shout ambles toward us with a full drink in his hands, spilling side to side. He clumsily sways out of the way of other tables and their guests, showing well how loose-limbed and drunk his stout self has become.

"Oh my, I'm sorry, sir. Let me…"

"Sit, sit, sit, my lady," he replies. "I'll get it."

He slams his mug onto the table and stoops awkwardly to collect his bag and the few papers that have fallen from it. He tosses it into the corner and finds himself a seat with us, brushing the hair back that has fallen around his reddened face.

"You were sitting here," Wilhelm says, starting to rise.

"I *am* sitting here, fellow," the man replies. "And you two are welcome to join me."

I exchange a glance with Wilhelm and he sits back down with a little smile.

The man takes a large slurp of his drink, and with his mouth buried into a lifted mug he asks something not understandable.

"Pardon?" Wilhelm asks.

He smiles and recollects with a long swallow of drink. "You good folks travel here to Boston, or is it your home city?"

Wilhelm looks toward me. "We'll be leaving tonight."

"Aye, good for you, good for you. I'll likely die here in this rat hole place."

"Are you sick?" I ask, shifting about in my chair. Something about being in a place of humans brings me some unease.

"Sick? No, not sick... well, in the head maybe."

"If you have such an aversion to Boston, you should leave," I reply.

"I wish I could," he says rather dramatically. "Alas, I cannot. I wouldn't live well in the woods. I am on assignment, you see. I have responsibilities to fulfill."

"To drunken yourself?" Wilhelm says.

"Ha!" He almost falls from his chair throwing his head back. "No, I'm afraid not. I represent reportings on the new colonies and must send monthly correspondences back home to England. This is my new home, but I am paid well and the ladies here are fairer than the maidens of the motherland so I will find a way to make the best of it all."

"You're a writer for England?" I ask.

"No no, for the *king* of England. He has his concerns about the settlements. Contrary to what the settlers think, he cares for prosperity to prevail here."

"I'm sure he does," Wilhelm says.

"Germanic are you then? Northern… Saxony I'll guess?"

"Brandenburg."

"Oh well, 'tis a beautiful land. And you, my lady?"

"Salem, but if I had to guess, I'd say my family was likely from England."

"Do you like it much in the village?" he asks.

"Not much."

"Aye, nor do I. Development is slow and this New England is hardly a place I see becoming prosperous for a long while."

"Why didn't you stay in England?" I ask.

"Ah, well, I am a bit of a fool and I got myself into some trouble back home. Needless to say, in light of my trespasses, I was offered a deal. A deal that was far better than prison, so I accepted. Though I question my decision sometimes."

Wilhelm and I look at each other, pondering what he could have done.

"I'm not a bad man," he says with a tone more serious than any of his others. "Tax related issues, ill business dealings – things that bring irony to my being here in the colonies. I may just leave though. Maybe travel the world and make up stories about new legislations, colonial jurisdictions and the like to send back home. Those idiots would never catch on anyhow. As long as the news kept coming to them, they would never question me. My reputation in England was quite solid you know – at least as a writer."

Wilhelm smiles. "We do not judge."

"Not church folk then, eh?"

"No." Wilhelm replies.

"Good, good. I had hoped the institution would lessen itself here, but the people of God have only become more eccentric, hanging folks and all. I expect that cruelty in England, but not here. 'Tis supposed to be a new land of progressions, aye? This tavern seems to be the only place in Boston that has any semblance of freedom, for the crowds can be rowdy and the ladies… well, the ladies are *quite* improper."

Wilhelm looks around, but in places far away. "I fear it will be some time yet before seasons change."

"I suppose you're right, my German friend." The man takes another large gulp of his drink. "Where are you folks leaving for tonight?"

"Your old home," Wilhelm replies. "London."

"You don't say!" The man gets wild-eyed for a brief moment. "Well, for what it's worth, I haven't been home in a very long time. My house is likely covered in plague dust, but I can give you the address if you good folks need somewhere to stay. Just clean up a bit, yeah?"

Wilhelm smiles at me. "You would offer your home to us?"

"Of course," he replies. "You are pleasant people and not rats. You are welcome to it. I own it still, but I'm not sure yet if I'm ever going back."

"We are very grateful for your kindness."

"Oh! I haven't even introduced myself! I do apologize, folks. My name is Percillus Crook, great writer for England." He pulls a paper, a quill, and a tiny bottle of ink out from his bag. He tears a piece off from the paper and scribbles onto it rather nicely given his state of inebriation.

"I am Wilhelm, and this is my lady, Verity."

"Oh, lady of truth, eh?"

Wilhelm smiles at me and nods.

Crook hands the paper to Wilhelm, then points his finger toward me. "Bring it to everyone, my dear. Too many idiots in the world today."

A woman suddenly appears over Crook's shoulder. I notice her eyes first, they look older than her face. She smiles politely at him, and emits a classy way about her. "I'm so sorry to interrupt you all, but I couldn't help but hear that you're a distinguished writer, sir." She holds a hand out to Crook, which he gladly accepts, pressing his lips to it for a long moment.

"I am indeed," he responds, "and are you as well?"

"Of course!" she replies. "What other career is so worth our work?"

"Your idealism is palpable," he replies. "What is your name, dear?"

"Anne," she says. "I've written many works that I'm looking for an editing eye to review – some poems, a dialogue on England, monarchy criticisms. I can pay whatever you'd like."

"Well." He stands himself up and finishes his drink, tipping his cup high and then slamming it down onto the solid table. "I'm sorry to leave you two, but I must be on my way, for the high ladies await my pen, and the street ladies await the graciousness of my wallet. Farewell, my German friend and his lady truth." He collects his bag and turns away from us with a comical salute, taking Anne's arm in his.

He leaves us and Wilhelm turns and smiles at me.

"He's an odd man," I say.

"But a smart one," he replies. "For he's a writer, a skeptic, and he knows the value of his freedom."

"If you say so."

Wilhelm stands up and extends his hand, helping me out of my chair and in this very small gesture, he's elevated my heart. Like a true princess I feel, if only for one powerful moment. "It's not too late yet if you'd like to visit the harbour."

"I'd love to see it," I reply, stepping through the doorway he has opened for me.

We move back into the streets of the beautiful city and I feel like we are a couple that has been together for much longer. I feel like years have passed because of the nature of our lives. The way in which I hold his arm as we walk, the way in which he looks down at me with adoration in his eyes. I think it all means more to him now, or perhaps he's just showing more than he did before. I think maybe we needed to be around humans again to feel these things in a human way. To appreciate for a moment that which does not last forever, even though we will.

I think this night in Boston has become the stage that presents our hidden feelings.

I think I love this man.

***

Enormous ships anchored at the entrance of Bendell's Cove loom like shadowy mountains over the sea. The wind swirls misty and the ocean lifts and dips the great vessels as it moves beneath them, bringing life to the massive structures. The waves break against the wooden pillars of the docks. There is a rhythm to this place and it is tranquil and dreamy and I can only imagine all of the stories that these ships would tell. It is surely one of the most beautiful sights I've ever seen.

"My father was a merchant," he says. "He was a hired hand for them I mean."

"Your father sailed these beautiful ships?"

"No," he replies, "he loaded wine onto much smaller ones. Back home there is a river called the Havel. He was a deck hand for boats that chartered the wine along the waterway."

"Did he ever take you with him?"

"Never," he says. "It was far too dangerous for that. He would bring home many stories to us though. He was a very imaginative man and always had a new one to share – sometimes true, sometimes not. I would fall asleep to him telling me about great battles with pirates or Lindworm serpents that were narrowly escaped on his travels. He would tell of their exotic swords, their blades rusted by blood, and frosty beards iced by a cold, villainous life at sea. He told of the golden glow from under the scales and the bits of tattered cloth of unfortunate travelers still in the teeth of the monsters. He always had something amazing to share. He wanted to be someone great for me and did not want to ever be thought of as lowly. Some men are content making a living by carrying boxes. My father was not that man. He had a storyteller's mind and an adventurer's heart and I believe he was meant to become more. I know he was."

"What happened to him?" The question releases slowly from my lips. I fear a sad answer.

"He was murdered." His gaze does not move from the ships before us and his voice does not waver. "By members of the Hanseatic League, a group that controlled trade in the region for a very long time. The League was dying during the time my father worked the waterways. While tied up in the harbour of the Elbe River, the ship was stormed by angry members who killed everyone on board."

I squeeze his hand a bit. 'Tis all I can do, for words will only get in the way of this moment. He is always so walled off, brimming with stories but never telling of them. I fear if I speak too much, I may end his seaside confessional and I have waited too long now to learn more of him.

"I was twelve years old," he says. "But I never knew what happened until I was much older, for my mother told me a different story. In keeping with his ways, she never told me he died. She spoke of how he was called to great traveling adventures. She said he would be gone for many, many years but that he would write to us and he did. The letters came every few months and I would revel in the stories with her as she read them to me. When I was four years older, my mother grew very sick and the letters stopped coming. I knew then what I had always suspected but I never asked her for the truth."

I look up at him. "Your mother sounds wonderful."

His gaze doesn't leave the spot where the ship masts meet the dark sky. Silence has crept back into him.

"Can I ask what became of her?"

After a pause he says, "Another time."

Not wanting to pry, I quickly change the subject. "Did you come here on a ship like one of these?"

"I've gone many places on ships like these."

I look away from him and out toward the rolling dark water. "Where was your favorite?"

"Here," he says. "I've lived the rich histories of the north and bared witness to the colored lands of the east, but their paths are written for now. Only here do I feel a sense of starting anew. We cannot fight the old. We cannot change traditions or cultures, but we can build new ones that will slowly begin to resonate into the new world and this is the place where it can be done."

"It begins with us," I say.

"Only us," he replies. "And then one day, the slow shift in winds will turn the distorted sails of the people toward the lands of truth, and all the starved peoples of the world will eat of its abundance."

I think of a long time from now, when the world will have its new ways. Rulers will die, old, yellowed books will rot away, and new ones will be written. Crisp, clean pages free of bloodshed pasts and coveted lies will replace that which will be buried in a dark history, never rising again.

Wilhelm kneels to the planked deck of the harbour, picking up something rounded and small, then rises, extending his hand. 'Tis an oak nut.

"You and I must first plant the seeds," he says, showing it to me.

I reach to him and cover his hand with both of mine; one under, one over, both tender upon the little symbol. We stare into each other's eyes for a warm moment, then a horn from a leaving ship bellows monstrously into the night. We both look toward the enormous wooden body moving out and away from the docks. The great sails have been raised and the wind's gusts blow them in and out in cascading rhythms, rising and falling like giant sheeted heartbeats, pumping life into the mammoth ship whose wooden, skeletal beginnings we hold together in the dark.

This little seed we hold.

ACKNOWLEDGMENTS

Firstly to you, I am so grateful that you shared in this little book with me. I wrote this story for all the beautiful young voices that hide silently away from the dangers and judgments of the world. I was once silent too, and it took me many years to master the confidence of honestly expressing myself, but life is far too important to be left to only the most poisonous tongues. Please remember that sometimes we all feel small, but even the flame of a single candle glows brightly across a sweep of darkness.

To Marah, Matt, and Julie, whom I met in my first creative writing class, your encouragements and friendships are the rarest I've ever encountered. Thank you for profoundly inspiring me in unwell times, and for the fun we shared in great times. I love you all. Carlon, your teachings were paramount in the undoing of my mind. Thank you for breaking me open. Nikki, no professional has ever pacified my fears of collaboration like you have. Your edits were extraordinary.

To my small but loyal circle of friends and family that never stopped encouraging me through the arduous work/life balance of completing a novel in the midst of this ever-so-unpredictable life. Your belief in me is so greatly cherished.

Dad, thank you for cultivating all the forms of creativity in your children, and for exposing me to so many varieties of art and entertainment (especially our movie nights). Some of my "storyteller" was born there.

Becky, for all you've done and continue to do. For your critiques, your enthusiasm, your belief in me, and for being my steadfast partner in raising our widdle wild one.

And lastly to my daughter, you are my absolute purpose and I love you wildly to depths that I could never fully express.

ABOUT THE AUTHOR

Jeff Severcool was born and raised in upstate New York, but resides in Charlotte, North Carolina. In addition to his writing, he's been active in a variety of martial arts for over a decade, and is completely addicted to tennis. He spends a lot of time Googling bizarre things for no reason – things like "Oakville blobs" and "Nicholas Cage's pyramid tomb." He also loves Zillow'ing houses he can't afford, loitering in coffee shops, and spending time with his daughter doing anything at all. *The Secret Witch* is his debut novel.

If You Enjoyed *The Secret Witch*
Stay Tuned for The Sequel…

Visit: www.jeffsevercool.com and follow the social media links for more info on upcoming releases, news, signings, or other random stuff related to Jeff and his writing.

Also, if you've somehow acquired this book for free, either through download or in print, please visit my website for a personal message from me…

CPSIA information can be obtained
at www.ICGtesting.com
Printed in the USA
FSOW01n0649210218
44854FS